I0733715

PULP LITERATURE PRESS

Issue No. 31, Summer 2021

Publisher: Pulp Literature Press; Managing Editor: Jennifer Landels; Senior Editor: Mel Anastasiou; Acquisitions Editor: Genevieve Wynand; Poetry Editors: Daniel Cowper & Emily Osborne; Assistant Editors: Samantha Olson, Brooklynn Hook, Veronika Kos, Melisa Gruger; Copy Editors: Amanda Bidnall, Mary Rykov; Proofreader: Mary Rykov; Graphic Design: Amanda Bidnall; Cover Design: Kate Landels; First Readers: Carol McCauley, Jessica Fabrizius, Jeya Thiessen; Subscriptions: Carol McCauley; Advertising: Samantha Olson. For advertising rates, direct inquiries to info@pulpliterature.com.

Cover painting, *Helby Island Afternoon* by Tatjana Mirkov-Popovicki. Artwork for 'Houses' by Matthew Nielsen. All other illustrations by Mel Anastasiou.

Pulp Literature: ISSN 2292-2164 (Print), ISSN 2292-2172 (Digital), Issue No. 31, Summer 2021.

Published quarterly by Pulp Literature Press, 21955 16 Ave, Langley, BC, Canada V2Z 1K5, pulpliterature.com, at $15.00 per copy. Annual subscription $50.00 in Canada, $68.00 in continental USA, $86.00 elsewhere. Printed in Victoria, BC, Canada, by First Choice Books / Victoria Bindery. Copyright © 2021 Pulp Literature Press. All stories and works of art copyright © 2021 their authors as per bylines.

Pulp Literature Press gratefully acknowledges the support of the Canada Council for the Arts.

Pulp Literature is a proud member of the Magazine Association of BC and Magazines Canada.

TABLE OF CONTENTS

Welcome to British Columbia!

Here in the northern hemisphere, the sun is high in the sky, the days are long and languid, the fruit is plump—and most of us aren't going anywhere. Yes, dear reader, it's time for another staycation summer.

And so, in the spirit of local living, I wandered around my memory and spent some time with my BC summers past. The highlights? Drinking well water for the first time and stalking ghosts on DeCourcy Island. Eating peaches fresh from the orchard and delivered by jalopy to an Okanagan campground. Building architecturally suspect sandcastles at Rathtrevor Beach. Camping on a seaside cliff top on Salt Spring Island, under giant red Mars. Introducing my kids to the kids in Coombs (Goats on the Roof—oh, please google this!). Buying a real-deal cowboy hat at a rodeo in Barriere. And so, so many more. My local summer-love list could fill this issue.

For many of us, summer season is road-trip season. Back roads, open roads, country roads, and pavement. And with me always, a book— my very own, portable roadside attraction. But well before the last page is turned, I'm already on the hunt for the next one. (Okay, who are we kidding? I'm *always* on the hunt for the next one.)

Fortunately, on every road trip, books abound. On rickety wire racks stuffed with cheap paperbacks at small-town pharmacies. In lovely independent bookstores in Tofino and Sechelt and Fort Langley. In used bookstores in Nanaimo and Victoria and Penticton. And on the creaking shelves of every town's church thrift shop.

So however near or far the winds of summer take you, we wish you great adventure — and happy reading. Because, as the bibliophiles among us know, when all else fails, *have book, will travel.*

~*Genevieve Wynand*

*I*N THIS ISSUE

'Helby Island Afternoon' by cover artist **Tatjana Mirkov-Popovicki** welcomes us to a bright day on the West Coast. However, we discover creatures lurking below the water's surface in feature author **Brenda Carre**'s 'Birdie' and **Colleen Anderson**'s 'The Search'.

Leaving the idyllic waterfront behind, we head into the city, where we encounter yet another creature in 'It Was a Chupi After All' by **Elsa M Carruthers**.

In **Graham Robert Scott**'s 'Armageddon by Tarantino', human monsters appear against the backdrop of the sky falling, and in SiWC runner-up **Janet Smith**'s 'Maslow Meets the Mayfly Moon', the ground falls beneath our feet.

We search for belonging and home in 'Houses' by **Matthew Nielson** and 'A Kinder Home' by **Hajera Khaja**. Allaigna and her companions also make their way back home in the final part of **JM Landels**'s *Allaigna's Song: Oburakor*.

In Bumblebee Contest winner **Alan Sincic**'s 'Blind Maggie', we learn not to mess with the titular heroine, and Frankie Ray puts the screws on her investigation in the last chapter of **Mel Anastasiou**'s *The Extra*.

The poems in this issue situate us firmly in place with vivid imagery of their settings. **Àkpà Árinzèchukwu** grounds us in the familiar hospital waiting room in 'Prometheus', and **Samuel Strathman** shows us the wild landscape from the viewpoint of the ground in 'Behind the Sumacs'.

Out of the fires of a Caribbean slave revolt, shipwrecked on the jungle coast of 16th-century Ecuador, an educated slave, a shaman, and a monk hunted by the Inquisition fight for freedom against the might of Imperial Spain.

Dive into an epic slipstream novel of intrigue and adventure from fantasy author Matthew Hughes, the writer George R.R. Martin calls 'criminally underrated,' and Robert J. Sawyer says is 'a towering talent.'

'A triumph!' - Cecelia Holland
'Sensational' - Candas Jane Dorsey

pulpliterature.com

Fantastic Fresh Fiction!

PULP Literature

BIRDIE

Brenda Carre

In addition to writing epic fantasy replete with intrepid female leads, tragic sorcerers, terrifying merpeople, and demons, Brenda Carre writes romance, science fiction, humour, historical fiction, and mystery. Her short fiction can be found in The Magazine of Fantasy & Science Fiction, Pulphouse Fiction Magazine, Heart's Kiss, *and in anthologies by* Fiction River *and* A Procession of Faeries. *Find Brenda on Goodreads and at brendacarre.com.*

© 2021 Brenda Carre

*B*IRDIE

On that wind-tossed autumn night off the coast of Inach Isle, the *Vision* ran aground on the Pinnacles. No rain — just a fetch like a fist.

Lord Calibari and two of his merfolk came that night to save me. Demons came too, as they will to a place of death and dying. As the *Vision* splintered down faster than a mind might believe, Calibari and his sisters defied death to pull me and three sailors to dry land with their strong-webbed fingers.

We were saved temporarily — if you could call it so — from the merciless hunger of the demons.

Yet I was pregnant.

Once ashore, grief-struck, terrified, I went into labour. The sailors who'd flotsamed ashore with me deserted. Base and miserable souls. I birthed my boy on the shingle there by the sea, on a bed of dry seagrass tugged from the high tide line.

Lord Calibari's two sisters shed their sea fins to help me, their green faces fierce in the light of a storm-angered moon. Calibari himself stood naked as a lightning bolt, watching for trouble at the edge of the seastrand, those rare-seen land legs of his a white glimmer in the dark.

I looked at the one sister as she gripped my shoulders. I saw the other's hands between my knees as she knelt ready to deliver my babe. I bit against a piece of manzanita driftwood and pushed my babe out.

His first wails were drowned by the roar of the waves and the scream of the wind beyond this haven.

He was born, ugly as a little rook, and already peckish.

"A lusty son," said my deliverer, her chuckle and hiss so like the tickle of the tide against the lee. She wiped him with seagrass, and her sister helped me deliver the afterbirth.

"We need to lead them astray—the demons," hissed that sister, so lithe and sturdy, muscled like a warrior, with breasts almost as flat as a man's.

The merwoman used a braided hank of my hair to tie off the cord. She used the blades of her teeth to bite into the cord and lift my son free at last. The cold salt of the sea stemmed my bleeding but dampened the seagrass they'd pulled around me.

Stars' Light, I was cold. Birth blood still soaked the shingle.

Of the afterbirth, the sister said, "We must take this through the swells to Judder's Point. Away—away, and leave it there. A chance it might lure the devourer demons there, and away from you and the babe."

A faint hope.

"I-I know," I stuttered, taking my son, now tightly wrapped in seagrass.

"We have honoured our debt to you, Birdie of Isla. We must go," she said, looking with surprising tenderness at my babe. Was she a mother too, I wondered.

I was a foster child to the Marshal of Isla when I'd revived an elder merwoman strangled in a fishnet, and kept her scales moist until her people came for her. That had been all of ten years ago. Even now I was little more than seventeen.

"Th-thank-k you," I said through clicking teeth. I needed a healer. I needed shelter and warmth, or my babe and I were going to die from exposure.

Calibari came to me now as the sisters left me. His hair was tousled wild by the hands of the wind. To me that wind smelled of iron and woe. Like his sisters, the merlord would need to return soon to the sea. He would wither and strangle without water.

With none to guide me, growing weaker with each breath in the cold, I struggled to nurse my newborn. His instinct knew better; he latched on with his hard little gums.

"A strong pup," said Calibari, placing a hand on my shoulder as my son took his first meal. The merlord's webbed fingers were the only warmth other than the burn at my nipple where my babe nursed fiercely.

"I could take him," he said with sadness. "It is in my power. Newborns already swim. It is just a small wriggle back to the sea. We would never steal a human pup, but with your word, I would save this one from the death that is coming for you. This boy is important. Save him for your world. I know who he is. What he is. All kin have waited, Birdie of Isla. We can take him. Keep him safe."

"M-m-make him merfolk?" I said, my breath hitching.

"No." Calibari coughed. He needed to go back to his element. "He will not be merfolk. He will breathe air and return to the land. He will only be ours for a time. This boy could save us. We would raise him to fight the demons that threaten us. Until then, let him be ours in heart and bond. Our sisters would nurse him and guide him to creep back on land when the time is right."

Already I was growing warm and sleepy, the tides of choice flowing away.

Let some part of his father live on. Let my son be hid beneath the sea, and when he's old enough, let him find a teacher worthy to build his powers . . .

"Take him. Keep my poor little hatchling safe. Hide him from the hunters from whom his father and I fled," I shuddered through stiffening lips. I wanted to ask him if my lover was dead. If our side was still chasing him or if they'd found him and sunk his ship. The OverSea would know. They would know I'd been on my own aboard the *Vision*. Whatever happens on sea or on the Isles, the merfolk know. The OverSea knows. Ah, but I'd left it too late.

I never felt the merlord take my son. With my babe out of immediate danger, I closed my vitals down into a death-like trance called the dark sleep. I was desperate to survive until someone should find me. Or not. At the mercy of weather and potential predators, I could not be certain.

I awoke with a girl's smoky fingers touching my face. Hot stones in blankets pressed around me.

An old voice was chanting: *dawn is coming, day is coming, horses run, horses run.*

The smell of sage reminded me strongly of clan rites my guardian had taken me to.

A healer had found me. Blessed Stars, I was found. Still so weak.

Then I went under again into a dream where demons ripped

at my flesh yet my flesh grew back. I still lived and searched for my son.

Up and down, as if surfacing on the waves and going under again, I fell into the dark sleep and back out again. Cold and hot, hot and cold. Rocks and water, steam and sage. I rolled in and out to that old shaman's voice chanting me back into life.

Dawn is coming, day is coming, horses run, horses run.

A face swam before me: a girl's, no more than fourteen or so. She was dressed in the grey robes of an apprentice adept. Her blunt, intelligent, plain little face was alive with excitement to see me waking.

I lay in a shaman's lodge — musty, close, and woodsmoke warm. Wooden rattles and bone rings and black and red regalia hung from a wall peg, and beside these were shelves of clay pots marked with sigils for healing.

"Huh! Huh," I said, trying to make my tongue work.

A very old man lifted me up from my pillow and gave me something bitter to sip from a treen cup. By the smell of the herbs upon his zigzag-patterned robes, I knew: here was the shaman.

The young girl leaned toward me and passed a small, cool hand over my brow.

"Can you hear me? You were in a shipwreck. You've had a child. My name is Kaii."

"Uhh," I said and faded once more, back into the dark sleep. A place of healing.

Even so, I heard her say, with some worry still in her voice, "The fever's broken, Master Ghut. Stones and Stars be thanked. Thanks to your medicine, I think she's going to live, but where do you think is the child?"

I was a long time coming back to life and not happy about it either. A few days after my fever broke, Ghut came in to find me struggling to get up, my wits still spinning and my knees like water.

"Peace, Daughter," he lisped through broken teeth and urged me back onto my pallet. "I did not save you to die on me now. You cried in your fever. You cried something of your son. We know why you grieve."

"The merfolk — they could be a long way from here by now."

He said something in his own tongue I didn't understand.

Seeing my puzzlement, he translated. "The spirit wills, but the flesh does not follow."

He pushed me back to the pillow. It was as if the old shaman saw into my heart. "You cannot find your son if you do not take rest. Not through mind or will. Better for the merfolk to hide the babe awhile. You need to spend a seven-day drinking mugs of broth to heat the blood and fire the limbs. This will help your body answer the will of your mind. Then we will see."

"See?" I said.

"If we can call your son home without the one who seeks you hearing us," Ghut said.

Just then the little apprentice came in with a full bucket of water. She thumped it down by the hearth and came over to us as if to sit.

"Child, your tasks are not done. We have a guest, and if you will remember, you are to heat water. Soak seaweed, grill wild onion, grind peppercorn," said Ghut.

"But—"

"Heat."

With a sigh, Kaii went back to the hearth. The old man winked at me. "For the next seven days I will teach you how our people heal."

So I healed in body if not in heart. I dreamed in the night of small fingers impossibly tiny and narrow, a touch so brief, so swiftly passing. I dreamed of the arms of my mate. Of his body wrapped warm around mine. I dreamed of Calibari and his sisters and a silver world beyond the reach of anything human.

Each day I woke a little clearer of mind, a little readier to stand, to mix, to sniff herbs for their proper savour, and to learn.

The two took turns keeping me company. Ghut's company was wise and knowing. "You should stay, you know. You *and* your boy, if we can call the merfolk to bring him back to us."

"I can't stay here. I have to get away, far across the OverSea. I'm like him — the Rev —"

"Shh." Ghut put a finger to my lips as the girl came in. "I think it's time to go on the sands tomorrow and call to the merfolk. What do you say, child?"

Kaii threw him a grin like the sun coming up. "It's about time, Uncle. You think I should fish us a salmon to celebrate?"

"I'll do it." He was already getting his pole and his bait bucket.

She plunked herself down on my pallet and sighed. "Nothing ever happens around here. The most exciting thing was finding you! You're on the run, aren't you? Tell me the truth. Are you a spy? Are you fleeing an unjust lord?"

"Losing a mate and a baby isn't mysterious enough?" I said.

"Feh! Who are you, Birdie?"

"I'm your friend," I said. But was I? Was I a friend of this child and her kindly old mentor? I was not if I drew them both into a war where nobody lives but the demons.

I did not dream of my child that night. I dreamed of the creature who'd betrayed me and the people of this country.

"Come back to me, I beg you," he said with that softness I so remembered. Teasing and winning me over to his lies.

A tallow dip glimmered, and Ghut's reedy query came to me.

"Daughter? A nightmare?"

"Yes!" I gasped. "My fault to put you at risk — both of you. I cannot call tomorrow. Better the merfolk keep my son safe. Our enemy will find me. I'm so sorry, Uncle."

"What risk?" said the girl, her unbraided black hair springy as a scarecrow's in the shadows behind Ghut.

He took my hand. "I can hide you."

"Even knowing what I am? That I'm like him —"

Kaii gasped.

Ghut turned to Kaii and his tallow dip lighted her small panicked face, the rumpled nightshirt, the knobby knees ...

"Your son must grow up to fight, not run. Let us teach him. Give him our magic as well as his own. Make it so the one you fear cannot fight him into submission. It can be done. You cannot run from this threat, Daughter. No sea is wide enough to get away. Only magic can fight magic. Tomorrow on the sands, Daughter, I will teach you how to make kelp salve. My apprentice has already gathered the kelp at my orders. Did you not, Kaii?"

She nodded, her eyes enormous.

"Who are you, Ghut, that you trust me so?" I said.

"I am a man of my people, just that," he said.

In the morning we kindled flame and Ghut threw the sacred powders upon the new fire, filling the air with manzanita smoke and sage, ambergris and nettle. This scented the place around us with a ceremonial gifting. Ghut donned the mantle of his calling to work his craft: his robe of woven brown and red zigzags, his amber beads about his wizened throat, an amber earring, and an eagle's primary in his hand.

"Be to me my centre, the Four Directions. The eye of power. Be to me the fingers of will. Be the stillness beyond thought. Be justice in the kill. The life, the truth, the seed within the flower."

I'd not heard this summoning before, yet it spoke to me.

The shaman stood, eyes closed, humming softly. His hum created an answering hum in my own body. I felt myself reflected as if in the glass of my own ocean. Not a monster but a reflection of power. I was running from that part of myself the Revenant wanted, and that was wrong. I had to learn, as Ghut said, to be more than the betrayer who had deceived me. Be more than the demons who could not be destroyed.

In that breath of time, I looked out to the world the shaman's chant had made new.

I now saw that the very same waters that had sundered me from my boy were also a part of his growing. Our world and the Stars lay in his growing. And in mine. The scent of sage and ambergris and nettle bloomed around me and into my resolve, wafting over me with each flick of the pinion Ghut waved over the smoke. I would do this thing: gather sea water and the kelp and render out the salve we needed to hide me from the Revenant. To keep his voice from teasing me to do his will.

Young Kaii tended the fire, chanting to the flames as she did so, and the shaman and I gathered kelp and driftwood. The fire rose and fell into embers that felt hot as a dragon's magic. We added the proper mix of herbals and sea water to the kettle and teased our kelp into fragments.

I remembered the song from the night I'd almost died. It had a hypnotic quality, one that blended with the time and tide.

Night is coming, light is fading, horses run, horses run.

Morning harkens on the morrow, sings the sun, sings the sun.

All that day we kept vigil over the kettle as the precious salve took on its magic. Sipping soup, we talked of life under the sun. The kelp paste rendered and the glorious scent of it wafted over the sea. The girl sat with us, sipping and listening. Her quick opinions had been outwardly stilled, but even so there was a knot to her dark brows. What troubled her?

I looked at the great open expanse of the OverSea where Calibari had taken my newborn.

Far away—but near enough to death for me to think it so. Calibari would not come tonight. Would he ever?

I would never have another child. There was a fragile comfort in me that my child was growing quick and whole and strong under the eye of Lord Calibari. I had made my choice.

"I will learn to make salve and drum the Stones alive that I may be a worthy healer in this place. I will stay, and learn from you, Uncle," I said to Ghut.

He scooped himself another mug of soup.

"This is a good thing. The people of Skyhaven, a day north of here, have need of a healer. But first, I will teach you to be a great one."

I stood up and bowed to him. "Thank you, Uncle. I will honour the learning."

I walked on legs that a few days ago had refused to hold me. The girl followed at a distance. Hesitant now.

She skipped stones into the glassy sea, hopping them like waterbugs.

I slowed my steps, and Kaii's hesitation to join me gave way at last.

"So. We can learn together, then," she said, a little sour.

"Do you wish it?" I asked.

She shrugged. "It is what it is."

"It might be what it is, but you don't like it."

She sighed. "The merfolk didn't come. Does this mean you're just going to let him go?"

Ah.

How could I find the words to explain how much my heart still ached? It would be a time yet before she even considered childbirth—and maybe never, given her calling.

"My mother gave me up, " I told her.

No answer. That knot of deliberation was back between her brows.

"I wondered all my life what could have caused her to do such an unthinkable thing."

I stared out at the sea and the clouded sun now low on the horizon. "This day will end with my arms still empty. Yet I was the one to let my child go, and for a good reason. I know that sometimes people have to do unthinkable things for unspeakable reasons, and my judgement of her all these years might have been wrong. I don't even know if she's alive or if she's not. But I hear her."

"So it's like she's talking to you now, sort of?" said Kaii, following my gaze. When she said things like this, it reminded me that she wasn't really that much younger than I. Three years at most.

"Yes," I said, surprised. "Or her ghost is." My eyes stung.

"I don't think she's dead, Birdie. Did the Marshal, your guardian, ever tell you she was?" said Kaii.

"Yes, long ago before he died," I said. "But I don't know what to believe anymore. Once you question the things you have always believed, you find it's not belief you need to question but *disbelief* you need to understand."

Every morning thereafter, we'd walk and search the horizon as those fishing ketches went out on seas that changed in mood with the clouds and the seasons. There was no sign until the day we gave Ghut his rites and sent his spirit to the Stars. On that gentle evening, as Kaii and I tended the burning by the strand for our gentle teacher, Lord Calibari and a clutch of his merfolk came to pay their respects.

The westering sun and the smoke from the pyre blurred them to my sight — awkward silhouettes upon land legs.

The toddler with them was yet more awkward on his spindles, but he ventured aside to chase gulls in an exuberant bout of exploration, unafraid upon the beach.

He gave a high-pitched squeal when a merwoman retrieved him. She picked him up, his hands tugging at her hair, and pointed at our fire.

I was running already, the wind a-sting at my eyes.

I felt myself a second star, incandescent with joy as our sun-star touched the sea.

Silhouettes resolved into naked green bodies, weedy tresses, muscled arms and shoulders, pale, thin land legs. One of the sisters was holding my boy. As she came to me with reluctance in her step, I saw that she had been the first to touch him and bring him forth from my body on that night the *Vision* went down. She had been his mother for a year and a day, and today she was making a choice to give him up.

My hatchling didn't cry when she passed him to me, and I cuddled him squirming in my arms. He was already warm, the whole of him shell-white and sandy as a pearl.

He didn't cry, though I must have seemed a stranger to him while that sister seemed his mother. But I did cry.

And so did she.

FEATURE INTERVIEW

Brenda Carre

Pulp Literature: *'Birdie' introduces us to the daughter of Gret, a witch we first met in Issue 15. Could you tell us a bit about how 'Birdie' came to be?*

Brenda Carre: First, I just have to say I adored S Ross Browne's stunning cover for Issue 15.

'Birdie' is one of those stories that was 'hatched' fully fledged. Call it a teaser entry into an epic fantasy mythos called the Chronicles of Ardebrin. Birdie (aka Starbird) is Gret's daughter. This short story introduces a significant future-shaping event that occurs at the end of Gret's novel — to be released in 2022.

The character of Birdie was born long before the character of Gret. Birdie first appeared in a much earlier iteration of *Father of Stars* (Book 3 in my Pendary cycle.) Birdie's protagonist debut came about as my short fiction often does: as a challenge to write a short story in one week on a specific topic. The topic in this challenge was to write an encounter where members of different races work together to change their world. This was one of those stories that wanted to be written and it flowed out of me during a Pulp Literature Hour Stories session.

PL: *What further adventures do you have in store for Gret and Birdie? Can you give us any hints about your new novel,* Gret of Roon, *to be released in 2022?*

BC: 'Birdie' is a teaser to *Gret of Roon* and an entry point into a mythic universe of novels where sleeping dragons govern the magic. In *Gret of Roon*, Birdie's mother joins forces with the ruler of Pendary (and the mysterious Revenant) to quell a rebellion and fight swarms of marauding demons. Hint: the secondary characters presented in 'Birdie' reappear in *Gret of Roon*. Infant Hatch's father appears as a secondary character. Little Hatch also makes an appearance at the end of Gret's book and grows up to become the protagonist in *Father of Stars*. The mysterious Revenant alluded to briefly has his own story in my current work-in-progress, *Son of Ravens*.

PL: *Place and world-building are so central—and essential—to your stories. How do maps figure in both your imagination and in the completed works themselves?*

BC: I adore map-making and have taught a class called 'Mapping to Story' at several conferences over the years. My Pendary books all come with a map. Our world is what it is now because of the stories of voyagers and explorers who sailed the seas and created maps. I studied physical geography in university, and out of these studies I came to realize how much a part of our environment we are, and how every part of a society is influenced by where we grew up and the obstacles placed on us by our setting.

PL: *As a writer of both short stories and novels, can you tell us a bit about your experiences working in each form, and how each might inform the other?*

BC: In 1994, while I was still at my day job, I began writing long fiction, which my agent was unable to sell. In 2006, I decided to move to writing short fiction in an effort to tighten my plots by taking 'smaller bites' at an idea. Keep in mind that short fiction has different parameters, but it still follows what is called the seven-point plot structure: character in a setting with a problem, three try-fail cycles, a climax, and a denouement. Short fiction follows one clear central objective that gets fulfilled at the end. Birdie has one clear objective at the beginning of her story that gets fulfilled with strong emotion at the end. Short fiction allows me to dive deep into a single powerful incident and get a more in-depth understanding of how a character confronts a self-changing event. For me, writing short stories deepens the characters so I can create conflict for them with the more complex plot threads of my novels. Secondary characters can show up in a short story that can also be written into a novel plot. So writing short stories has definitely helped me become a better novelist.

PL: *As an artist and visual arts educator, what are some things you enjoy most about creating in different mediums? How do art and writing collide for you?*

BC: Prose and poetry, like the visual arts, have shape and form, and when the proper tools of the craft are used with artistry, the medium produces a dream-like state in the reader/viewer that absorbs them entirely in the image and emotion. Art and writing for me collide in ways that would take me an essay to explain. I'll put it down to a few words here: I am sucked into my medium with passion and fear of the unknown because, when they converge, something new appears that is always a revelation.

PL: *Do you have any writing or visual arts mentors? What advice have they given you?*

BC: I have been blessed by my mentors. In the visual

arts, they were Sam Black, Tony Onley, Gordon Smith, and the many educators and studio artists I have worked with, especially my teaching partner Karen Brumelle (brumelleart.com). And of course by my very creative students who in so many ways taught me more than I taught them. In my writing career, I credit so many professional colleagues and friends: Dean Wesley Smith, Kristine Katherine Rusch, Carol Berg, David Farland, Kevin J Anderson, Rebecca Moesta, and Donald Maass. I could continue far longer here than I have space to write names. Over and above all, I credit my sister Mary Kennedy, who believed in my art and shared her own with me. We were each other's muse.

PL: *As a mentor yourself, what advice would you give to writers and artists just starting out?*

BC: Same advice as my mentors gave me: face your fears because inside fear is passion and revelation. Don't fear failure. Failure can be the path to knowledge. Just create and grow — it doesn't have to be perfect; it just has to be finished. That's how we learn.

PL: *Where is your favourite place to write? To draw and paint?*

BC: I create in my office, sometimes at a desk in the bedroom, sometimes in the breakfast nook where I can look out on the water. Currently I'm not painting but working on story maps, drawing character sketches and cover designs, and using my phone to amass a folio of imagery to use as ideas for settings and characters. I do have an external workshop for 'smelly' work and sometimes I paint out there or do furniture restoration. More about how I work, and some imagery, can be found at /brendacarre.com.

PL: *Thank you for taking the time to speak with us. Before we go, one last question: In addition to your new novel, what are you working on now?*

BC: Thank you so very much for giving me the opportunity to share my world with you. I'm working on the first draft of *Son of Ravens*, which I hope to release after *Gret*'s debut next year. Not long after that I hope to release Hatch's book, *Father of Stars*. There will be more short fiction set in my universe as well as more novels. I also write short fiction in other genres. To quote Kevin J Anderson, co-author of the *Dune* series: 'the busier you are, the luckier you get'.

THE EXTRA: FRANKIE RAY MAKES MURDER'S FINAL CUT

Mel Anastasiou

Mel Anastasiou writes mysteries, including the Fairmount Manor Mysteries and the Hertfordshire Pub Mysteries, available at *pulpliterature.com*. For her novel Stella Ryman and the Fairmount Manor Mysteries, *Mel won a Literary Titan Gold Book Award and was longlisted for the Leacock Memorial Medal for Humour.*

© 2021, Mel Anastasiou

The Extra:
A Monument Studios Mystery

Movie star and thwarted director Marietta Valdes has just confessed to murdering matinee idol Gilbert Howard. Frankie Ray should be happy to hear Marietta admit to the crime for which she herself stands accused, but Marietta is an excellent actress and a fluent liar, and her confession doesn't add up. What's worse, nobody knows better than Frankie that the electric chair waits off-set for the real murderer, so she'd better get it right.

We discover Frankie, still disguised as that handsome private 'tec and male ingenue Frank Achilles, in the ashes of the burned-out movie set, putting the screws on her investigation.

Chapter One

In the silence that followed Marietta's confession, Frankie noticed that moonlight turned the actress's dress and lips grey, so that she appeared more than ever her screen self in the black-and-white world of the movies. And despite her skilled delivery of the line "I did it," Frankie was certain Marietta was acting. Lying.

Was Marietta capable of murder? *Abso-tively.* Marietta was capable of anything in the pursuit of her career. Frankie had never met anybody so ambitious in her life. But capability was not enough.

Marietta had no motive to kill Gilbert Howard.

Frankie said, "Marietta, it will be as obvious to the police as it is to me that you had no reason to kill Gilbert Howard. He was your only ally in your struggle to direct *The Emperor of New York.*"

Eugene scowled. "Yes. For once, try to control your need to be the centre of attention, Marietta."

"It's my *job*," Marietta said bitterly.

Frankie made a strangled noise in her throat that turned into a smoky cough. And she coughed again. She'd coughed so much since Marietta had dragged her out of the fire that by now her throat felt as rough as the gravel under her feet.

"Eugene knows every word I say is true," Marietta insisted. "I killed Gilbert Howard."

Eugene shook her head. "I killed him."

Frankie snapped a look from Eugene to Marietta. Then she raised her gaze to the heavens and wished she'd never met either of them. Of the three people sitting here, exhausted in the aftermath of the studio fire, one was lying about being the murderer. The second was lying about *not* being the murderer. And the third person — Frankie herself — was being sought by the police for the murder. For Pete's sake.

She said, "You're knitting a story out of pure deception, aren't you? Like screenwriters write movies. Your story is a fake."

Eugene said, "Everything in Hollywood is phony."

"Hollywood," Marietta said, "is a law unto itself. It is also the axis of the spinning world."

"I'm sick of all the lies," Frankie said.

"Look who's talking," Marietta retorted. "You've told at least three since I dragged you out of the fire. And you call yourself a gentleman."

Frankie looked down at herself in her man's clothing. "I'm really not so much of a gentleman as I appear to be."

"That's all right," Marietta said. "I'm really not much of a lady."

Frankie nodded. "This particular lie ends right here. Marietta, I'm not Frank Achilles. I'm Frankie Ray, dressed up as a man like Eugene here, in order to clear my name of Gilbert Howard's murder."

With vigour, and with a maximum of modesty in the circumstances, she wriggled the Xeno-Flex Combination down from around her middle, over her hips outside her trousers, and down to the ground. And what a relief that was. She took deep breaths of the smoky air while her rib cage expanded like a bellows. She desired nothing more than to stomp the Xeno-Flex into shreds. However, she reminded herself that the garment belonged to the Queen, now recovering from her attack in hospital, and she ought to return it undamaged.

"Frankie Ray?" Marietta stared. Then she laughed. "You really are the biggest liar here, then. Maybe you did kill Gilbert Howard after all."

Eugene let out a quiet groan. "Shut up, Marietta. I've put Frankie here in mortal danger, and we owe her at least the good manners not to joke about it."

Frankie said, "You owe me more than that. You owe me the truth. Tell me what happened that night. Eugene, exactly where were you when Gilbert Howard was shot?"

Eugene looked up at Frankie. "I was with you, Frankie. I was dancing the carioca with you. Don't you remember?"

Frankie did. She recalled everything about that first night at Paradise Villas: the music turning on the Queen's gramophone, the velvet warmth of the air, the young women and men winding a conga line under the stars, and the cracking noise that had sounded like a gunshot. It really was a gunshot. She had danced with Eugene while Gilbert Howard was dying.

She said, "One of you, tell me what happened to Gilbert Howard."

Eugene looked at Marietta. Marietta looked at Frankie.

"I will tell you." Marietta got to her feet and stood in front of Frankie and Eugene. She said, "Picture the scene."

"I can't. I wasn't there. I was *dancing*," Frankie said bitterly.

"Pretend it was a movie." Marietta smiled. "You watch movies all the time, Frankie. And I know how to make them, so I'll make this one for you."

"Please tell me, straight out, what happened."

Frankie might as well have begged night to turn to day. Marietta would do things her own way. She always had, and Frankie bet she always would.

Marietta began, "Here's the set-up for the action. It's a story of three girls from Eugene, Oregon, who came to Hollywood and met a famous movie star. Gilbert Howard helped one of them to a career in the movies—"

"That was Marietta," Eugene said.

"He sent one of them to hide in a brothel until a movie deal might be made for her—"

"That was Billie."

"And he fell in love with the third."

"That was me." Eugene swallowed hard. "I couldn't find Billie when she ran away to the brothel."

"Why a brothel?" Frankie answered her own question. "I see. It's the perfect place to make Leo, who loves her, feel as badly as possible for not making his parents help her in the movies. Why didn't Gilbert Howard help her instead of hiding her?"

"Howie was always unpredictable," Marietta said. "And he liked his little joke on King Samson, hiding his son Leo's true love in a brothel."

Eugene nodded. "I followed Billie's trail as far as the Garden of Allah. There I fell headlong in love with Gilbert Howard. And then I lived as a man so that I could visit Gilbert often without harming his Don Juan image."

"If only love had changed Howie that much," Marietta said.

"It did. He was happy with me."

"Was he? There were lots of other girls."

"Yes. He couldn't be happy if he had to leave other girls alone."

Marietta's expression softened. "He was crazy about you, Eugene, no matter how many girls he was with. Listen, Frankie, and I'll show you the scene. I'll be the camera."

Marietta tipped back her head as a light breeze picked up the smoke clouds and wafted them away over the studio walls. Frankie knew perfectly well how much Marietta was enjoying her audience. She leaned toward Frankie and Eugene, eyes flashing.

"This story goes to the root of storytelling, back thousands of years, when *what's at stake* was formed out of an ancient idea of Hell …" Marietta was wearing her director's face again, with its wild objectivity that made Frankie try like the furies to understand every word. "Even today, our lead actors must escape from Dante's condition: *alone in a dark forest.* I will tell you what happened that night."

At last. Frankie leaned forward as Marietta began to describe the events leading to the death of Gilbert Howard. When Marietta spoke, Frankie saw the scene as if from the front row of a cinema, a bag of sour lemon drops in her hand, and her eyes glued to the silver screen.

Fade in.

The scene: Gilbert Howard's well-furnished living room in the Garden of Allah. Outside the window, the night is dark but for the brilliantly lit swimming pool.

Our star performers, Marietta Valdes and Gilbert Howard, appear in the window. To the cinema audience, at first the scene between the two actors looks like love: the first clutch of romance.

In this way the camera proposes the cinematic question: Will the desirable Marietta Valdes give way to Gilbert Howard—a true Don Juan!—when she has always been so careful to keep him at arm's length?

But he, who has offered to help her become a film director against all the odds, now threatens to withdraw his support. Will Marietta submit to this man of perfect beauty and complete determination in order to further her career?

She will.

She will not.

Marietta resists; Gilbert Howard persists. He threatens her, mockingly, with the gun he found by the bushes at the edge of the property.

She doesn't laugh. She pushes past him toward the door.

He shoulders her away from the door and takes her in his arms. He believes he knows better than she what a woman really wants. And he is expert at pushing his luck.

She pushes back. They struggle, and she catches hold of the gun between them. His expression changes from amusement to anger.

We hear the first sound from the screen: a shot rings out.

Now the viewpoint character is revealed: the slim blonde woman attired in men's clothing. Eugene emerges from the shadows to see her lover dead on the floor. Her friend Marietta stands over him.

Fade to black.

Marietta sighed dramatically. "I was only going to use the gun to force Howie to let me go. In a way, he shot himself, although my finger was on the trigger."

Frankie said, "That's a pretty neat way to describe a murder."

"Good point." Eugene rose to her feet. "And you got the timing terribly wrong in that scene, Marietta."

Frankie remembered that first night in Paradise Gardens, dancing the carioca with Eugene Ellery. She remembered the backfire noise that sounded like gunshot.

Eugene must have been remembering that moment, too. "I wasn't standing at the window while you shot Gilbert. I was dancing with Frankie. You ran over to my villa after Paradise Gardens had settled down for the night. You woke me up to tell me he was dead."

"What matters is the truth of the story, not the facts," Marietta said. "A director's reputation relies on logic in narrative, not accuracy."

"Shut up if you can't tell the truth, Marietta," Eugene said.

"All right, but only because I'm thinking," Marietta replied.

Eugene turned to Frankie. "These last few days, I decided I would never leave Hollywood, because I feel close to Gilbert here. But it's clear that I can't stay."

"Don't you dare talk like a martyr, Eugene," Marietta warned.

"I'm not a martyr. I'm a realist. It was my fault that you killed Gilbert, Marietta. If I'd been with him, he wouldn't have tried to seduce her, Frankie. Marietta would never have shot him except in self-defence. I loved Gilbert—"

"Gilbert Howard. A man who simply took what and whom he wanted," Marietta interjected.

"Yes. I accepted his weaknesses when I accepted his love. I should have protected Marietta from him."

"You should have protected every girl he seduced and then abandoned," Marietta said.

Eugene nodded. "Maybe. But instead I let him have his wandering way."

"You're still taking the blame for his behaviour," Marietta pointed out. "You should have grown up a little by now. In fact, for a satisfying narrative composition, you should have transformed *before* the showdown."

"Maybe this conversation is the showdown." Eugene scowled. "Anyway, I am stronger now. Gilbert's dead, and I have nothing to lose. That's why I'm going to take the blame for you, Marietta. I should have done it from the start."

"I've told you a hundred times to keep out of the whole—" Marietta began.

"But I'll have to leave Hollywood." Eugene looked ready to cry once more. "I had planned to visit Gilbert's grave every day. But Eugene Ellery will have to disappear. Eugene will take the blame for you, Marietta, and Eugene will clear Frankie's name as well."

Marietta shook her head. "You're a fool, Eugene. Even when you were Elaine, you were a very silly girl."

"Sure. How else did you and Billie talk me into coming to Hollywood when I didn't care a cent about the movies?" Eugene rose from her spot on the plinth. "I'm going to miss you, Marietta. And I'm truly sorry about getting you involved, Frankie. But this will pay for all."

Her pale, cropped hair shone white as snow against the shadowed walls and dark skies as she paced along the path leading through the sound stages to Sunset Boulevard.

Frankie rushed after Eugene and caught her by the shoulder. "Why, Eugene? *Why* did you dig up Gilbert Howard's body from your backyard and bring it into my house? *Why* did you have to leave him with me?"

Eugene paused. She pulled herself free. "Respect," she said. "Marietta wanted to bury Gilbert quietly so that everybody would think he'd simply disappeared because he was so unreliable. I thought it would be enough to keep him near me, under the grass behind my house. But Gilbert was a movie star. I couldn't leave him there. I loved him too much."

Frankie began to see. "And he loved fame with all his performer's heart."

"Gilbert would have hated to disappear without giving the world a chance to mourn him. When you and I were in the backyard, looking at his body lying namelessly in the dirt, you spoke to him with such respect, even though you didn't know who he was. You believed he was a poor old uncle." Eugene's eyes shone with tears. "I knew you were the right one to find

Gilbert's body properly—to call the police and the newspapers and see that he was honoured. I'm sorry that it all went wrong, Frankie. I'll put it right now, as best I can."

Eugene turned again to leave. Frankie took two steps after the slender, retreating figure. Then she stopped. She had nothing more to say to her. So she watched Eugene—Elaine—Ellery walk away with a step so light it seemed as if her bones were hollow, like a bird's.

Frankie turned back to Marietta. "She shouldn't be alone."

"There's a lot that *shouldn't be* in this great big story of life. For example, I don't like the end to this particular scene, do you?"

Frankie followed Marietta's downward gaze. There on the plinth, ready to the actress's hand, lay King Samson's gun. The gun Frankie had dropped on the set of *Ambition*. The gun she'd believed to be lost in the fire.

It shone silver in the moonlight and contained, Frankie well knew, one remaining bullet.

Chapter Two

Almost home. Eugene leaned against Frankie's car and gazed up at the sign that read Paradise Gardens. *She felt exhausted after the night's exertions, transformations, and unhappy revelations. A reflective moment on her own was all she wanted in the world.*

No. She was putting off the moment when she would have to shed her pretence at being Eugene Ellery. In a way, it would be like losing a friend.

On the floor of Frankie's Model A, Eugene spotted a small dark shape. She leaned inside and picked up a woman's squashy tam, discarded and bereft. It would be just the thing to cover her head when she stopped being a man and

became a young woman with very short, bobbed hair. She twirled the hat on the end of her finger, wondering what else she would lose when she parted with Eugene. But having lost Gilbert, nothing else mattered.

Without further delay, she passed through the gate into Paradise Gardens. It occurred to her that the murdering criminal mastermind John Dillinger carried a ten-thousand-dollar reward — alive. A reasonable reward for Eugene, supposed killer of one movie star, ought to be around five thousand. But with such an international case, she bet that Gilbert Howard's accused killer would soon rank no lower than third on the Most Wanted list.

It was a pretty funny outcome for a girl who never wanted fame. She ambled along the path between the bungalows at Paradise Gardens, enjoying the swing of a man's walk for the last time. At home, Eugene slipped out of her suit and hung it on its wooden hanger in the closet — the closet where Eugene had created a hiding place for her women's clothing. The same closet where Frankie had hidden after first being accused of killing Gilbert. Eugene smoothed the collar of the grey suit as it hung empty, the way the Queen had smoothed it the first day she'd helped Elaine become Eugene.

"Confuse the senses," the Queen had said, handing Eugene a tube of Burma-Shave. And the Xeno-Flex Combination! After the first few days she'd given that torturously constricting garment back to the Queen and worn her jacket buttoned. She knew the Queen had passed the Xeno-Flex on to poor old Frankie.

How Marietta and the Queen had laughed the first day she went to look for Billie Starr and fooled the ladies at the brothel, even though Billie had refused to answer her door. How Eugene had cried the second day, once she'd met Gilbert Howard and fallen in love for the first time in her life. Against all the odds, he'd admired her above all the others. Little Elaine Ellery! It seemed impossible until she saw what pleasure he took in searching out the woman underneath the man's disguise. Gilbert loved that he was the only one who knew what Eugene really was.

For love of Gilbert Howard, Elaine had pretended to be Eugene Ellery, here in Villa 7A. Now, for love of Gilbert, she would leave this place forever. Faithful from first to last. Loyal to her true love and loyal to her lifelong friend, Marietta, who had shot Gilbert dead. Eugene knew such blind allegiances were her weakness, but they also served as a shield against grief.

She clicked the boards out from the back of the cupboard and peered into the dark space behind. She hadn't envied Frankie her night hiding inside it, but it had kept the girl safe.

She reached into the dark interior of the cupboard and gathered the armful of women's clothes she'd folded and hidden away the previous year, when she'd begun dressing as a man. She ought to air them and iron them, but she didn't have that much time. She'd just iron her travelling dress.

Funny to think that since she'd become a man, she'd grown much better at ironing. It was those darned collars. Gilbert had taught her to iron her shirt collars first. So she ironed like a man, the way her lover had taught her. Eugene Ellery was faithful to the last in matters great and small.

Even on that horrible night when Marietta shook her awake to confess that she'd shot Gilbert and needed her help, Eugene hadn't lost her centre. She'd stayed calm while helping wrap her lover in his bed sheets and, with Marietta, dragging him behind Villa 7A and burying him in secret. Then she stood sentinel at his grave all night long, leaning on her shovel for support. But when dawn struck, she'd recognized her error in burying him without any marker, any mourners, any news reports of his tragic death. How he would have hated that particular anonymity. Gilbert Howard loved drama.

So she dug him up. Inch by exhausting inch, she'd dragged him in the sheet all by herself across the yard to Villa 7B. The steps at the back were the worst, but when she'd finally wrestled him onto the sofa and cleaned him up, he looked so well that she knew it had all been worthwhile. A pity about all the trouble it caused Frankie. Setting it up so that the true-hearted young Canadian, Frankie, would find Gilbert and see that his passing was properly honoured had been an error, certainly. But there it was: Elaine—Eugene—had lost her own true love, and she wasn't thinking straight. Still, she'd done one thing right. Gilbert had been discovered the way he'd want to be, sitting up and dominating the news reports.

She wiped a tear away and decided to leave Eugene Ellery's grey suit where it was for the police to find.

I must do three things quickly, *she told herself.*

First I must write out a confession, telling how I 'shot' Gilbert Howard.

Next, I will sign it *Eugene Ellery, Howard's most loyal fan.*

And finally, Eugene Ellery will disappear forever.

Eugene looked into the mirror and said her true name aloud: "Elaine O'Leary." *Tonight her name sounded like a lie, but she would grow accustomed to it.*

Elaine.

She pulled on the squashy tam she'd taken from Frankie's car. She reckoned she'd have three weeks of hiding her hair under the tam before it grew back to a suitable feminine length. Her throat hurt, and she saw her reflection crumple and waver as tears rose in her eyes.

She mustn't cry. A weeping woman attracted help, and she must pass unnoticed. She was a woman wearing a hat, no different from a thousand others.

Soon, Eugene Ellery's face would be on the wall of every post office across the United States. Everywhere, four sharp tacks would puncture her picture, while across the bottom it would read:

Eugene Ellery. Wanted for the Murder of Gilbert Howard.

Their names would be joined forever. That would go a long way toward making this past year worthwhile.

In the pocket of her travelling dress she found a coral lipstick. She uncapped it, applied the lipstick to her mouth, and blotted it with the back of her hand, the way women did. It was all coming back to her now.

Chapter Three

Scraps of flame red edged the movie-set walls. The last of the firemen had left the square. Frankie and Marietta sat alone together in the shadows. If the plinth underneath them had been real marble, it would have been too cold to bear. But as it was plywood painted to look like marble, the seat was tolerably comfortable.

Marietta set the gun down on her right, out of Frankie's reach.

Frankie said, "So you really did kill Gilbert Howard."

"At last you believe me. It's about ruddy time."

"I believe that you killed him. But I don't

believe you killed him in order to protect yourself from his unwanted advances."

"And you accuse *me* of not listening? You must remember what Eugene said. And what I told you."

"I was listening, like a good little moviegoer." Frankie shook her head. "And you directed the scene very well. But that wasn't a newsreel you showed me, Marietta—it was a movie story you made up."

Marietta rose from the statue plinth the way a queen would rise from her throne. She gazed down her nose at Frankie.

Frankie stood up and placed her hands on her hips. "You always knew what Gilbert Howard was—a womanizer. A seducer. And maybe worse than that. But he was your only important supporter in your struggle to become a director. You forgave Gilbert Howard for betraying your friend Eugene over and over again with other women, and you accepted him sending your sister Billie to a brothel—"

"Billie didn't sell herself!"

"Exactly so. Therefore, you lied to Eugene about why you shot Gilbert Howard."

"I'm a very good liar." Marietta inclined her head. "And let's be honest here: you're almost as good a liar as I am, Frankie. Passing yourself off as Frank Achilles."

"At least I have a good reason."

"I have a better reason."

"For killing a man?"

"Of course. You said it yourself—I'd make a great director." Marietta scowled.

"Yes. I believe you could do it."

"Not only me. Understand that I don't want to be the only

woman director. I want to be the first of many women to direct a major motion picture. You're ambitious. You understand. I thought that Howie understood, too. But I was wrong."

Frankie stared. "Are you saying that Gilbert Howard turned against you? He'd stopped supporting your cause with King Samson?"

"I confronted Howie. I said he was a turncoat. A traitor. He told me I was gorgeous when I was being ridiculous. I couldn't direct a movie. All I could do was be beautiful, and that should be enough for me. It was certainly enough for him. *Excuse my little white lie,* Gilbert said." Marietta blinked her lovely eyes. "He laughed."

Frankie understood more than Marietta had perhaps intended to reveal. King Samson had called Marietta a virtuous woman. He had meant *difficult to seduce.* In other words, a pleasing challenge to a womanizer like Gilbert Howard.

Frankie said, "When you turned your nose up at Gilbert Howard's advances, he laughed at you. He'd only backed you to direct *The Emperor of New York* in order to make you grateful?"

"So that I would come to him."

"Make love with him."

"Yes. Gilbert Howard viewed me not as a talented director but as a challenge. As a notch on his romantic bedpost."

For a moment Frankie feared that Marietta would break out crying. She would do it beautifully, too, the tears streaming down her ivory cheek, shining in the night.

But Marietta didn't weep. She said, "When I first arrived, Howie showed me the gun he'd found in the bushes between the Garden of Allah and Paradise Gardens. He set it down on his sofa table between us. When he laughed at me, I picked up the gun. I meant to kill myself." She looked ironically at Frankie. "I know you don't believe me, but it's true. But then as I was steeling myself to do it I thought, the world has so many Don Juans, doesn't it?"

"And so few talented female directors." Frankie shook her head. The fact was, Marietta's reasoning was correct. Not moral—not even human—but correct.

But that didn't change a thing. The woman was a cold-blooded murderess. Justice had to be brought to the case. Frankie had to go—leave the set, leave Monument Studios—now, before Marietta figured out what a threat Frankie was to her and her ambitions. Because Marietta could hardly direct a film from prison.

Frankie looked at the gun lying at the foot of the statue, pointing her way. Maybe she ought to make a grab for it. Now, while Marietta appeared to be lost in thought.

Marietta picked up the gun. "I wish you really were Frank Achilles. I could have used you on my side."

Frankie gazed at the gun. She wished she were Frank Achilles, too, because a man might have a chance of wresting the gun from Marietta. A man would probably have taken the chance the first moment he saw it.

Frankie said, "I still believe you'd be a wonderful director."

"Thank you. And what about you? You're an extra again."

"I was the pigeon girl," Frankie said. "You helped me get that role, remember?"

"I probably do remember," Marietta said, "but I can't think about that now."

She shifted the gun from one hand to the other.

"You can't shoot me. Not after saving me from the fire," Frankie said. "Not after making my dreams come true by helping me get a chance at my first speaking role as the sad manicurist."

"I have a mathematical question," Marietta said.

"I teach mathematics," Frankie told her. "Not past sixth grade, though."

"Answer me this, then. How many people would I have to save to make up for killing just one?"

"I don't know," Frankie said honestly.

Marietta wrapped both hands around the gun's grip. "I would have saved you a lot of trouble, wouldn't I? If I'd done what I'd intended and killed myself instead of Howie. If I'd remained true to what I know: that life, like filmmaking, is narrative, and storytelling requires your characters to struggle against the odds."

"You still can," Frankie said. "And I think you ought to."

"You would! Because you've struggled against the odds, Frankie. I wish I had followed my first instinct and shot myself instead of him."

Frankie's mouth felt dry, and she found it difficult to speak. "Gilbert Howard had no right to force himself on you, no matter what else your ambitions were telling you. You can explain about that when you turn yourself in to the police. I can find other girls to back up your story."

"I will never turn myself in. And I won't allow you to turn me in, either."

Marietta took a deep breath.

Frankie stayed absolutely still. Her thoughts were racing, and the loudest one was, *What a waste, if she shoots herself!* A waste of youth, life, and talent.

Frankie remembered Gilbert Howard's laugh, and the way he swung out his arms as if to embrace the whole world, whether it wanted to be embraced or not. All his talent and charm weren't enough to save him.

And maybe Marietta's talent and charm would prove equally useless.

With a sudden leap sideways, Frankie threw her full weight at Marietta. They fell onto the gravel together. She and Marietta struggled for control of the gun, while its muzzle slewed wildly back and forth across the set, now pointing at the smoky wall, now at the sound stage, now straight up at the statue of the horse and rider. Frankie hauled harder against Marietta's grip. At the same time, Marietta seemed to grow stronger. Frankie remembered that this Oregon beauty had grown up playing with the boys. Between tomboy Marietta and Frankie the substitute schoolteacher, who would win out?

"Stop!" Frankie said. She shouted right into Marietta's ear, and the actress's grip faltered. Marietta pulled the gun free, and Frankie let it go. She scrambled backward, crab-like. "Wait a minute."

Marietta, gun in hand, pulled herself up to sit with her back against the statue's plinth. She pointed the gun at Frankie.

Frankie said, "Marietta, you killed him. You're going to have to …" What was her father's word? "You're going to have to make up for killing him."

"Atone?"

"That's the word."

Marietta looked down at the gun. "What better atonement?"

"Shooting yourself is not atonement. It's the easy way out."

"I don't know the easy way to do anything." The gun wavered. "All I know is that I committed murder."

Frankie stepped closer. "What about Gilbert Howard's crimes? Years of them?"

"True. But is the world a better place now that Gilbert Howard is out of it?"

"No," Frankie admitted, but added, "Maybe it's better for all the women he would have bullied and seduced."

"He was a talented man, and that talent has certainly improved the world."

"The world of the movies, anyway." Was that enough? Frankie let out a strangled cry. How was a person supposed to judge anybody? Judicial robes, clerical robes, or no robes at all, the thing was impossible. With a suddenness that was almost frightening, Frankie lost her taste for justice.

She said, "You're going to have to give me King Samson's gun, Marietta."

Tentatively Frankie reached out a hand. When Marietta didn't step back, she took hold of the muzzle and tugged at the gun in Marietta's grasp. She half expected it to go off, but this time Marietta let it go without a struggle. Pointing the gun carefully down at the gravel a few feet away, Frankie fiddled with the mechanism that opened the chamber in order to empty it of its one remaining bullet.

"I hate this gun." Frankie stopped fiddling with the chamber and got rid of that last bullet the natural way, by firing it straight up into the air.

Marietta jumped. "For heaven's sake, Frankie!"

"I really do despise this gun of King Samson's. But it's got one more job to do — for you, for me, and for Gilbert Howard." In her imagination, her father's voice added sternly, *To make amends for its misdeeds.*

Marietta frowned as Frankie tucked the empty gun into her pocket. "What are you going to do? I won't go to jail, Frankie. I won't."

"Be quiet, Marietta. Let me think what to do and how to do it. Because this gun of King Samson's has got to atone."

Chapter Four

Frankie stood alone in the backyard of Villa 7B. She had hoped to have an orange for her breakfast, but the tree was bare of fruit. After the two most gruelling and dangerous days she had ever spent, she couldn't believe how disappointed she was that somebody had harvested every single orange. Furthermore, a mouse had found the half-empty bag of bread that Frankie had left under the orange tree the evening before, when she'd slaked her hunger before following Marietta into the fire. She brushed the morning dew off the bag and put a finger into the little hole in its side. How Connie's mother would shriek if she saw that a mouse had nibbled at it. And Champ's mother would about drop dead.

No, there was not an orange to be found in her own backyard, but at least the place was blessedly empty of police.

Frankie scrubbed away a yawn and wiggled her bare toes in the spiky grass. One could buy an orange, or bread not nibbled by mice, *if* one had money, which she did not.

In fact, the problem of money for gasoline for Frankie's drive home to Vancouver was being addressed, although not by Frankie herself. Right now, Tom was somewhere nearby, a cup of cooling coffee in his hand, strolling from bungalow to bungalow. He was gathering coins for Frankie's trip home. Nobody at Paradise Gardens had much to give, Tom said, but everybody had something.

Tom and the kids were real troopers. She wished she didn't have to leave them.

She carried the bread inside, past the rubbish bin on the back porch. There, peeking out of the top of the bin were Frank Achilles's suit and shirt, neatly rolled around the battered Xeno-Flex Combination. She had decided not to return any of it to the Queen. Hollywood was complicated enough without any more of the Queen's transformations.

Frankie had made one exception to the purge of manly wear. The sunglasses Billie had stolen, which had so neatly distinguished Frank Achilles from Frankie Ray, lay nestled in Frankie's skirt pocket. She was keeping them because she liked the way she looked in them. And because she wanted to remember that not everything about Hollywood was tainted by ambition and greed. In her other pocket she carried King Samson's gun, because she was certainly not going to leave it lying around the place for anybody else to find.

She decided she ought to say a polite goodbye to Connie. But Connie wasn't at the table in the living room or in the kitchenette. Frankie peered into the bedroom and then the bathroom, but she was nowhere to be found. So her former friend hadn't even bothered to wish Frankie a swift *bon voyage*. Well, that was just one more bridge Connie Mooney had burned behind her.

Frankie set the loaf on the table and cut the nibbled corners off two pieces of bread to make toast. One slice fit into each side of the toaster. While they cooked, she attempted to imagine being back home in Vancouver, with her father calling for his tea and Champ whistling along the lane, swinging a milk bottle in one hand. No matter how hard she tried not to, she pictured Doris leaning in the kitchen door of the blue house in Vancouver, wanting a gossip. When she tried to imagine the vegetable truck trundling up the lane, she envisioned Tom on the back steps of her father's house, gesturing widely with his piece of toast so that he knocked the red geranium off the porch rail onto the grass below.

She flipped the toast slices over to the uncooked sides. When she snapped the toaster closed again, the diamond chip on her engagement ring, back on her ring finger, caught the light from the window. She set the pot of gem-red jam onto the table.

Steps outside on the pathway sounded like Connie's, moving at speed. Frankie remained unaffected. She opened the toaster and spread jam across each piece, not neglecting the edges. There was still no butter in Villa 7B, but there would be lots at home in Vancouver. She took a big bite of toast and closed her eyes so that she wouldn't see Connie come in.

At a nasty-sounding slap on the table, Frankie opened them again. A folded newspaper lay on the table next to the plate of toast. Frankie glanced down at the front page. There, above the fold, her own face stared back at her. Frankie shook her head in disbelief. The newspapers ought to have heard the news of her innocence by now, because Eugene had promised to deliver her written 'confession' to the police before she disappeared forever. Was every promise ever made in Hollywood to be broken? She made a little noise of despair.

Behind her, she heard the tap of an impatient foot. Frankie scraped more jam onto her toast. She would not turn around.

Connie said, "You are so stupid."

Frankie would have let her know that calling people *stupid* had no effect on their actual intellectual capabilities, but she doubted this information would do Connie any good, so she held her tongue.

"Frankie, look at the headline." Connie snatched up the paper, turned it over and dropped it back onto the table. Frankie stared down at *The Los Angeles Morning Gazette*, Blanche Carver's paper. Before she could curse the columnist's duplicity, Connie read the headline out loud, her delivery as clear and crisp as ever.

Witch Hunt for Innocent Woman
Called Off

Innocent woman. Frankie felt a buzzing in her bloodstream. As the feeling rose, she wanted to rise with it, to dance barefoot around the room. She would like to tear out of the house, calling for all of the Queen's kids to come and celebrate with tea and toast and gem-red jam.

"Still giving me the silent treatment, I see," Connie said. "You know what? You're a completely different person since you came to Hollywood. It doesn't suit you, either. I should have left you behind in Vancouver, where you belong."

Entirely composed, Frankie bit neatly into the toast. She read the second, smaller headline, centred under the first.

Maniac Fan Confesses
Killer Eugene Ellery Remains at Large

And Eugene Ellery would remain so, since he no longer existed. Only Elaine remained. Frankie sent her a heartfelt thanks for keeping her word after all.

But how interesting that Blanche cleared Frankie's name in the larger headline. One would have thought that *Maniac Fan Confesses* would have been the editor's choice for the top line, as a far bigger incentive to sales than a simple clearing of Frankie's name.

Connie said, "Yep, Hollywood's changed you, all right. You used to be kind and friendly, and now look at you. The silent menace."

Connie pulled three oranges out of her pocket and dropped them into the blue bowl sitting on the table.

At last Frankie broke her silence. "You stole all the oranges from the tree out back."

"It's my tree," Connie retorted.

"No, it's our tree," Frankie reminded her.

"Not anymore. You're driving our car back to Vancouver."

"My car."

"Your dad's car."

"And you stole it! Like the oranges."

Connie leaned across Frankie and seized the second piece of toast. She took too big a bite for manners. Connie said cheerfully through a mouthful of toast, "Yes, Hollywood, city of dreams, has turned you into a movie villainess. Theda Bara could play you, if she acted a little nastier."

Maybe Frankie had changed, for she met this supremely unfair accusation with a private accounting: *I saved the Queen, I saved Billie, and I saved you, Connie Mooney.*

What was more, she longed to explain that she was certain that Blanche Carver had placed 'Witch Hunt for Innocent Woman Called Off' as the top line under the *Los Angeles Morning Gazette* because Frankie had saved Blanche, too. The headline was the columnist's apology to Frankie. She considered revoking her silence long enough to explain the concept of regret to Connie, who wouldn't know an apology if it trotted up and whinnied for attention, but decided against it as too esoteric.

Frankie bit into the last burnt corner of her toast. She was about to rise when Connie dropped a folded blanket onto the table. "If you're leaving tomorrow, you can move your bed out here tonight." Connie said. "Your breathing keeps me awake, and I don't suppose you know how to stop."

Frankie turned and looked Connie in the eye. "Do you remember when we were thirteen and you talked me into forging a letter to excuse us from a Math test and then bragged about it?"

"No."

"No? That's very interesting. We were both caught and subjected to the most unfortunate scenes imaginable at home and at school. What about the time you cut my father's front door mat into twenty pieces and sold them as bits of flying carpet, and I got switched for it?"

"No."

"Well, Connie, these are no longer important incidents when compared with the events of the last forty-eight hours, but they are certainly representative. I can think of a hundred betrayals and a thousand burned bridges and not one single, solitary apology from you."

"You ought to write a book about it. Say, you'd never believe who's living in sin next door in Eugene's old place, 7A." Connie raised her eyebrows. "Billie and Leo. I guess it's practically married life compared to what she's used to."

Frankie would have smiled, had she been a little crueller. "They *are* getting married," she told Connie. It seemed like a good exit line. Far better than farewell. She wanted a cup of tea, though, before she snapped her suitcase closed for the road. "Billie's trying out for a part in *The Emperor of New York*. I had a screen test set up for this morning for a small but good part, and I'm going to give the chance to her. Billie knows what to say to the director so that he'll give her the chance instead of me."

Billie was to tell the director that she was the pigeon girl.

The pang she couldn't help feeling at giving away her own audition would subside over time. She hoped. After all, Frankie couldn't have her cake and eat it too. She couldn't win the part of the sad little manicurist *and* go home to marry Champ. Still, it was nice to know that if she had taken up acting as a permanent career, she might have known some small success. She wondered whether her children would listen with interest to her tales of Hollywood life, even if they were romanticized and exaggerated: *And there were real oranges, hanging right there for the picking, outside my back door.* But children are never much interested in their parents' lives, only in their own adventures. Frankie wondered how she would feel in twenty years when a daughter of hers and Champ's climbed out of a bedroom window and went off without a word to find her fortune.

Out in front, a flurry of pigeons landed in the centre of the patio, where later on the Paradise Gardens kids would get together and put on some music. Maybe Tom would light a fire in the oil barrel and the air would fill with the aroma of sausages. She smiled when she remembered the lights shaped like parrots, and decided she would buy some bird lights to string on her Christmas tree when she was married.

With a start, she saw that while she was dreaming, Connie had filled the kettle and made tea.

Frankie looked from the blue cup in front of her to the square of toast by her right hand, to the stack of money on her left. This stack had quietly appeared when she was thinking about the birds.

It looked a lot like forty American dollars. A bolt of anger flashed through her.

She picked up the money in both hands and held it to her breast. "You stole my money, Connie! It was you all along."

"That cash wasn't safe under the sofa cushion." Connie dropped her eyes and fiddled with the knob on the toaster. She burst out, "And you're so *stingy* with it. Our first day on the movies, and you wouldn't bring a thin dime with us! I took it because I thought we might want to celebrate. Or buy something for this place. Butter for the toast, at least. Well, your money's all there."

"Is it?" That was something, anyway.

"Of course. You think I'm Bonnie and Clyde?" Connie fished in her pocket and brought out a few bits of change. "Well, almost all the money is here. I bought a pair of stockings and a Coke when I was driving around with King Samson."

On the top bill—a fiver—Frankie saw something shiny, right under the motto *In God We Trust*. It looked like a drop of water, round and flat.

"You're crying," Connie said.

Frankie touched the second drop of water that had fallen beside the first on the five-dollar bill.

Frankie rarely cried. She had always believed that was because, no matter what happened, nothing could be worse than losing her mother. And compared with what she'd been through over the last few days, she had nothing at all to cry about today. But as she sat at the breakfast table eating toast with her former best friend, Frankie's eyes pricked and swelled behind her fingers, and tears streamed down her cheeks, wetting her palms and running along her chin and down her neck.

She buried her face in her hands and felt the tears run through her fingers.

Connie, the uncertainty plain in her voice, said, "Everything's all right now, Frankie."

"No, it's not. It's not all right, and it never will be again."

Outside there was a bustle of wings. Frankie looked up through her tears and saw the flock of pigeons take off and fly away above the roofs of Paradise Gardens. The bougainvillea waved as they passed. It was time for Frankie to leave, too. She ought to pack her things into the Model A and leave right away.

Still, she sat and wept. "Oh, Connie, I've been so awful. I took Champ's ring off after I promised I wouldn't, and I was going to hock it."

"Well, it's really not much of a ring," Connie pointed out.

"I ran out on my father and didn't even say goodbye. When my mother did that, he took to drink and got defrocked. And I left your mother to deal with my dad."

"My mother's a big, grown-up girl," Connie said. "And you know how your dad always lets you get away with murder, stealing the car all the time and everything."

Frankie sobbed harder. "I let Marietta get away with murder. I found out she shot Gilbert Howard, and I didn't turn her in to the police."

Connie blinked. But she said, "The only reason Marietta would shoot Howie would be to defend herself. So, I think that letting Marietta get away with it was a sweet thing to do. Seeing that nothing could bring Howie back."

"*Sweet?*" Rubbing at her eyes, Frankie shook her head. "It wasn't sweet. She killed him in cold blood, and I let her go, because—"

"Because you didn't want to send somebody you knew to fry in the electric chair?" Connie asked.

"No."

"Anyway, you oughtn't to help those darned police, the way they treated you. But what if they figure it out for themselves? Will you lie for Marietta?"

"No. Yes." Frankie stared up at Connie, who would never be able to understand the real reason she had let Marietta go. "The thing is, what if I turned Marietta Valdes in for murder and they executed her? Connie, if that happened, then all those people would have been right. I would have *killed a movie star.*"

"Gosh." Connie stared. "That's a pretty good reason, I guess. But that's not why you let her go."

"Yes, it is."

"Nope. I know you, Frankie Ray." Connie leaned in closely. "One thing about you, Frankie, you're fair-minded. And you pay your debts."

"So?"

"So, Marietta saved your life in the fire. And you saved her life from the electric chair."

"Maybe." Frankie wept some more. "I guess I've burned all my bridges all over Hollywood."

Connie emitted a long sigh. She moved her chair closer and hugged an arm around Frankie's shoulder.

"Well, Frankie, if there's one thing I've learned in life, you can burn all the bridges you want, and they always grow back."

"Oh, gosh, Connie. I'm sorry," Frankie sobbed. "I'm so sorry."

"It's okay, Frankie." Connie patted Frankie's shoulder. She moved Frankie's money out of the way of her tears and poured another cup of tea.

CHAPTER FIVE

Half-hidden by the bougainvillea that grew beside the front gate of Paradise Gardens, there was set into the stucco wall a metal mailbox with a flap. The mail was collected at two o'clock sharp, and it was nearly lunchtime. Frankie lifted the mailbox flap and felt in her skirt pocket for the letters Connie had urged her to write home. Careful not to pull out King Samson's gun, which she was still carrying for safety, she pulled the letters out and looked at them. She had written them that morning, Connie had licked the stamps, and Frankie had sealed and addressed them.

The first letter contained her letter of resignation to the Vancouver School Board.

The second letter, written to Champ, ended her future as a woman married to a man with a perfect soft mouth she loved to kiss. This envelope also included her engagement ring, wrapped in tissue paper.

The third and last letter was addressed to her father. It was a valedictory to evenings in Sheridan D's company, laughing with her father over Jack Benny on the radio; a goodbye to fond good-nights and promises of tea in the morning; and an unwritten but implicit farewell to the vegetable man with his rattling truck bearing beets and carrots to every housewife on Thirty-Sixth Avenue.

She let the mailbox flap drop and put the letters back in her dress pocket next to King Samson's gun. She would not post them after all. What was Hollywood compared to family, true love—whether it was Champ or another fellow—and neighbours like Hazel to help Frankie raise her children? Instead of letters, she would send herself home in the model A and claim her future in Vancouver. She had the whole drive northward to figure out whether she would end her engagement to Champ. One thing this trip had taught her: there are possibilities everywhere, and a woman could choose among them as she liked. She did not have to sit around, hoping to be chosen.

She was glad to be friends with Connie again, but that did not mean Connie should dictate Frankie's future, no matter how hard she sold a life in Hollywood to Frankie.

Frankie felt decisive, now, and completely in control of her own future. She determined that for lunch, she would make exactly three cheese sandwiches: one for Connie, one for herself, and an extra one in case Tom dropped by. There was not much cheese in the packet she'd bought at the corner store, but it would be enough to share among friends. Later tonight, there would be sausages on the fire and dancing around the dry fountain. And tomorrow, or perhaps the day after, she would say her farewells and drive her father's Model A home to Vancouver.

Frankie turned her back on the mailbox. She was halfway to the Paradise Gardens gate when she heard her name called in full, first and last.

"Francesca Ray."

"That's me," she said. *It is I*, the past and future schoolteacher inside her whispered. The detective movie star she had become over the last few days laughed silently, rocking on his heels.

She turned to look. Right in the middle of Sunset Boulevard, King Samson braked his car and climbed out, letting the engine idle. The big car stood shining in the sunlight, its engine muttering to itself while cars honked and drove around it.

King Samson walked through the traffic as if he were walking on water. A sports model nearly ran him down. "Goddamn it all." Samson turned and raised his fist. "You don't own the road."

"I guess I own as much of the road as you do, buddy. Move your car," the driver retorted.

With a rude gesture, King Samson angled his wide body between the Model A parked at the gates and the runabout in front of it. He walked up to Frankie at the mailbox and said, "Marietta Valdes says that you've got something I want."

"Hello to you too, Mr Samson." Frankie tipped her head a little to one side. She'd rolled her short blonde hair into pincurls and tied it up in a scarf. Tom said it suited her, so maybe she'd keep the platinum as long as Champ didn't object. It would remind her of her triumph as the pigeon girl. Billie Starr had gone ahead and taken Frankie's place at the audition for the sad manicurist. Frankie didn't have a doubt in the world that Billie would get the part. "What could little old me have for you?"

King Samson peered at her. "You look familiar."

"I drove you from Oregon to Los Angeles," Frankie said. "You did warn me that you don't have a memory for faces."

"I sure do remember those two girls who drove me to Hollywood. A redhead to die for, and a schoolteacher type." Samson scowled. "You don't look like her."

Frankie touched her pincurled, platinum hair. "Nothing is as it seems in Hollywood."

"You said it, sister," Samson agreed. "Now, down to brass tacks. Where's Frank Achilles?"

"Retired from the business, I hear," Frankie said evenly.

Samson scowled. "Frank Achilles has got a responsibility to Monument Studios and *The Emperor of New York*."

"He might be hard to find." Impossible to find, actually, since Frank Achilles—embodied as he was by his clothing—remained curled up in the garbage bin by the back door of Villa 7B. All of him except his sunglasses. Frankie slipped her hand into the skirt pocket that didn't have her three letters or the gun in it and rubbed her thumb across the lens.

"None of your impudence. Get me Frank Achilles." King Samson turned red around the ears. Frankie took a step back, but with the wall behind her and the big man in front of her, there was nowhere far to go.

She smelled the coconut pomade in his hair. She raised her right hand, hesitated, and then placed it flat against his lapel. "You'll never find him. Frank Achilles is gone forever."

"But I'm cooked without him," Samson said.

Frankie looked King Samson in the eye. Poor old King Samson. He had only his hard heart, money, and power to get him through each day. She, on the other hand, had some very good friends who could use her help. She patted Samson's lapel and bowed to the inevitable.

"Well, maybe I can track him down, so long as we can work something out. I've got a few things to trade." She would have to be careful not to let Marietta's secret out. Very careful indeed.

She reached into her right-hand skirt pocket. With a glance around to see that nobody was close enough to see her, she pulled out King Samson's gun. It felt by now as familiar in her hand as her teacher's blue correction pencil used to feel. She looked down at it. He looked down at it, too. She said, "This gun …"

"Yes?" He stepped toward her.

"It's yours?" She peered up at him. "Is it the one your wife gave you?"

"Of course it is," he said. "Look at the crown engraved on the grip. It's one of a kind. It's mine. Give it to me."

Frankie nodded. "I will. With great pleasure, believe me. But first, I'm afraid you're going to have to make a choice, Mr Samson."

Samson growled, "Exactly who do you think you are, anyway?"

"I'm nobody," Frankie said quickly. "Just a Vancouver girl, and you're a self-made man. I've not accomplished very much in my life so far. But even so, I'm afraid that you really need to decide something: Do you want to know about this gun, or don't you? Do you want to know where it's gone, and what it's done?"

King Samson stared from her to the gun. Frankie watched as his face transformed from anger to frustration to understanding.

Gilbert Howard himself, with all his acting genius, couldn't have made his feelings clearer.

"No," King Samson said. And again, more heavily. "No."

Frankie nodded. "That's how I feel, too. Because it's already done enough damage. Here. Take it."

King Samson took the gun from her. "What do you want?"

"I want you to put it on your mantelpiece, locked up behind glass or something."

Samson gave a sharp nod and slipped the gun into his pocket.

Frankie said, "About time. Now, down to work."

"What does that mean?" King Samson raised a thick, well-groomed eyebrow. "Blackmail?"

Frankie almost laughed aloud, because she actually had considered blackmail. Considered and rejected it. There was enough dirty work going on around Hollywood without her adding her two cents' worth.

"Mr Samson, you told me that you are looking for Frank Achilles. I know for a fact that Frank didn't sign a contract with you," Frankie said. "Why do you want him, anyway?"

"*I* don't want him. He's unreliable." Samson said. "But Marietta wants Frank Achilles. She ran the footage that she took of the fire for me, and it's better than anything else we got last night. Damn her. So I'm going to let her direct a scene. *One.* One scene only. And she insists on using Frank Achilles."

Frankie rolled her eyes. Trust Marietta Valdes to get it all wrong. Frankie had wanted help for the Paradise Garden extras, not a part for her own discarded alter ego. With a sigh, Frankie began pulling the pin curls out of her platinum hair. She slipped the bobby pins into her pocket as she spoke. "I guess you'll be going back to your wife now, Mr Samson?"

"Sure, I'd go back to my wife," he said, baring his teeth. "*If* she hadn't moved in with her golf pro six months back. Listen! Give me Frank Achilles's agent's number. I don't need to waste any more time with you."

"No, I guess not." She combed her fingers through her short hair to loosen the curls. It was time to lay her cards on the table. "But you do need me to keep another secret if you want Frank Achilles. And this one I do want to negotiate."

"You?" King Samson stared. "Exactly what has Frank Achilles got to do with you?"

Frankie pulled out the sunglasses out of her pocket and put them on. "That's what," she said. "Let's talk."

"*You're* Frank Achilles?" King Samson stared, then dragged the palms of his hands across his face. "I hate this business."

Out on the street, the cars complained, passing Samson's abandoned sedan.

"It must be very difficult to be you," Frankie agreed. "Come on. Park your car properly, and let me make you a cheese sandwich."

Frankie held the door open for King Samson. He hurried past her, late for his early afternoon casting meeting at Monument Studios before a three o'clock shoot. In one hand he carried an extra cheese sandwich Frankie had cut for him, and in the other the list of demands that Frankie insisted upon. It was a short list, but it had punch.

She shut the door behind him, rinsed King Samson's plate at the sink, and set it on the drain board.

She had negotiated well in a tight spot. Now she made a particular effort not to think of any further demands, because that would be taking advantage. And she would keep her part of the bargain right now, before the long drive home. She was perfectly happy to do so. She could hardly wait for this afternoon's shoot.

Frankie smoothed down her platinum hair with Eugene's Burma-Shave and wished her former next-door neighbour well, wherever she was. She stepped into Frank Achilles's pants one leg at a time. Leaving the Xeno-Flex in the bin with those three letters, she buttoned up her men's jacket and set her sunglasses on her nose.

She strolled out into the patio area by the fountain and called all the extras at Paradise Gardens to gather round to hear what she'd negotiated for them. They massed around her and listened with noisy pleasure for the good news she had to tell them.

A cheer rose into the hot Hollywood sky.

Frankie was not at all sorry that there would be one last gasp for Frank Achilles before he disappeared forever out of Hollywood. King Samson was not the only one who ought to pay for unwittingly providing Marietta with the gun that had killed Gilbert Howard. Frankie, too, felt the need to atone, and that was why she had agreed to be Frank Achilles one more time for the camera. She would play Marietta's sweetheart at the beginning of the movie, not to be seen again until the end. Two scenes for Frank Achilles. It was the least she could do to help out poor old King Samson.

"Follow me, kids," Frankie said.

She led the way among the bungalows toward Sunset Boulevard. As she passed the orange tree in front of Villa 9A, Frankie plucked an orange from its twig as if it were opportunity itself, juicy with promise under the thick skin necessary for happy survival here in Hollywoodland.

She pressed the orange against her lips—a kiss for good luck—and then tossed it up into the air. Connie caught it. She tipped the orange to Tom, who threw it over his shoulder to somebody farther back in the crowd. Frankie didn't look back to see who caught it—somebody caught it, she was sure, and somebody threw it again, even though over the noise of the kids chattering and laughing she couldn't hear the slap of palms against the fruit. This wasn't a moment for looking back. This was a day for marching onward. This was a day she'd never forget, no matter how long she lived her life in Vancouver.

Tromp, tromp, tromp went the footsteps of the little army of extras, with the quick counter beat of Tom's steps as he scurried to catch up to Frankie and Connie at the front of the troop. He hooked one arm through Connie's, his other through Frankie's, and for no reason but high spirits, the three of them laughed fit to bust.

But they didn't stop. They'd never stop.

The script was in her man's jacket pocket, and Frankie rehearsed Frank Achilles's first lines in *The Emperor of New York* in her head. *Don't leave, my darling. Never let me down.*

Never let true friends down. Right off the bat, she had made Samson agree that the Paradise Gardens extras would have lots more work. And she hadn't forgotten the Forgotten Man—she'd sent word to the doorman at Camillo's to meet the crowd of them there so that he'd have a little part, too.

Frankie's second demand was screen credit for everybody. Gosh, how King Samson hated that one.

Her third and penultimate demand of King Samson regarded Billie Starr. *Make sure that your daughter-in-law is welcomed into the family. Talk to Blanche and make her listen, too.* Billie would have Frankie's part as the sad little manicurist. And Leo would have Billie.

So far, success.

But it wasn't success that mattered most. Most important were these uncertain moments before you succeeded—when you still could lose, but you wouldn't. Frankie's final demand was that Marietta Valdes direct the first and last scenes of *The Emperor of New York*. And she would bet her nearly forty dollars that Marietta would end up directing more scenes than two by the time filming was done. The world would have its first famous and respected woman director, and more of them would follow. That was Marietta's atonement: to help other women direct motion pictures. Unbidden, the thought occurred to her that if only Frankie stayed in Hollywood, then maybe, just maybe, one of those woman directors would someday be Francesca Ray herself.

Frankie laughed out loud in her Frank Achilles voice. She hadn't wanted to be Frank anymore, but she adored taking big manly strides and laughing from her diaphragm. Good old Frank Achilles. He was not long for this world, but while he still existed, she decided to enjoy the fact that her alter ego was a very popular man.

The day expanded like a hero's chest and shone like a heroine's smile. It was as warm as the final kiss, the fade out, and *The End*. Let the credits roll with a roar of timpani or trumpet! For up there on the screen, an actress would read her own name among those unfurling white on black or black on white. When she saw her name she would know—posterity would know—that she was *here*. In Hollywood. And Frankie's name, with all the others, would live forever on that bit of clattering celluloid. One film before she went home. This one film.

Tom gave a hopping skip that knocked both of them sideways. They might have fallen, but Connie, laughing, pushed them back onto their feet. Frankie put her hands in her jacket pocket and found three envelopes tucked in there. Connie must have put them there. Frankie pulled them out and stared at the three letters she thought she'd left in the garbage bin back at Villa 7B. Three letters saying that she was not coming home. That she was staying in Hollywood. Three letters she had decided not to post.

Or had she? At what point was a decision made? Did thought or deed constitute resolution?

It was a few minutes yet to two o'clock, when the mailman would empty the box. Frankie turned and ran back against the tide of excited extras to the mail slot in the wall outside Paradise Gardens.

She rested the envelopes in the iron mouth of the postal slot and noted how white they looked against the black iron, and how blue the ink appeared against the white.

She dropped Champ's envelope into the mailbox. It made a whispering sound as it fell. And as of that moment, she was no longer an engaged woman.

The draught from the passing cars rippled her dress at the shoulder blades, tucking her skirt between her legs. She removed the second letter and let it fall in with the first. The Vancouver School Board would hardly shed a tear at losing her.

She held onto the third letter a little longer than the first two. It was addressed to her father, and contained an invitation to visit her and see Hollywood with his own Vancouverite eyes. She would never tell him how cross she'd always been with him that her mother had run away. And her father would never recount how tough it was to be left alone with a toddler, trying to keep his little girl on the straight and narrow. But she knew he missed her like she missed him.

The third envelope followed the first two down the rabbit hole. She felt a sudden chill and wished that she had not been so swift to post them. She might be able to get them back. She could squeeze her hand partway into the slot and catch the corner of at least one of them between her fingers and pull it back out.

She shoved her hands deeply into her pockets. It was illegal to interfere with the mail once posted. She now saw that this was a very good law.

Frankie hesitated, gazing along Sunset Boulevard at the other Paradise Gardens extras walking ahead of her. She was their leader, and it would not do to let them get too far ahead of her. Still, this moment of import deserved some kind of recognition.

She raised three fingers to touch her forehead below her platinum hairline. Frankie snapped a Girl Guide salute at the mailbox, and ran off to join the rest of the extras marching toward Monument Studios.

§

Want more Frankie Ray? The Extra: A Monument Studios Mystery *by Mel Anastasiou will be available as a full-length novel in print and ebook from Pulp Literature Press this summer.* pulpliterature.com/product/the-extra/

PROMETHEUS

Àkpà Árinzèchukwu

Àkpà Árinzèchukwu is an Igbo writer. Their work has appeared in the Kenyon Review, Prairie Schooner, the Southampton Review, Poetry Review, Adda, Fourteen Poems, Arc Poetry, Clavmag, the Lumiere Review, Trampset, and elsewhere. They were a finalist for the Black Warriors Review Fiction Contest 2020.

© 2021, Àkpà Árinzèchukwu

$\mathcal{P}$ROMETHEUS

At the hospital's waiting room where no one
finds love, it feels the Eagle, a thousand years old

might have been drunk on a feast of this immune
system. It is just six months after the first detection,

I am seeing from the eyes of others lovers who have run
because what can't be explained in plain English is better

left unattended. Like what is the word for a mother's silence
when she heard the Lord had done his thang?

The virus at its spring, too early for little showers
should not get me worried. But since I have lost

interest in all earthly things, Lord, I just want to talk.
Of course, as usual you could choose to not talk back,

but I know what I want: a life free from worries; a sun above me
but never too ambitious with regards to consuming this

reckless body of mine, which you might think is preposterous
considering I gave a man the fire he burnt his son with.

At the hospital's waiting room where the doctor meets me,
Lord, your mercy endures forever: that the machine has seen

where I have refused to look a part of me too long dead for salvation.
Looking at the ceiling which is equivalent to looking onto God

I hold a man in my embrace, he flutters into unwanted memories.

A KINDER HOME

Hajera Khaja

Hajera Khaja's fiction has appeared in Joyland, TOK Magazine, *the* Humber Literary Review, The Puritan, *and the* Journey Prize Stories *anthology. She lives in Mississauga, Ontario, and is currently working on a short story collection.*

© 2021, Hajera Khaja

A Kinder Home

For as long as I can remember, Ammi and Abbu had talked about leaving India and settling abroad, and whenever they brought up the various options — Chicago, London, Singapore, all places where we had some family — I was the only one who felt apprehensive, a burning feeling settling in the pit of my stomach. These were places where I felt I would be swallowed whole, engulfed in a horde of pedestrians or struck down by a rush of traffic, places where I would no longer have any sense of bearing and feel forever lost. So it came as a surprise to me that I felt no panic or anxiety when one day, as he was sipping his afternoon chai in the wicker chair by the front door, Abbu announced to us that he would try for Canada. I had no knowledge of the place; I had not read any books or watched any movies set in Canada, but I liked the sound of it, the syllables plain and unadorned as if offering comfort through its relative anonymity. My younger sisters, Aziza and Shaista, who were ten and six at the time, were less pleased. At once they started bombarding Abbu with questions about why not America or England, and where was Canada even, and how come they had never heard of it. Abbu said Canada was a kind and safe place where immigrants were welcomed. He also had a second cousin there, Safiya Aunty, who had moved to Toronto in the seventies, just three months after she got married. That was the time it took in those days for a visa to be issued to a spouse. It was a much longer process for us. For weeks, we ate on the ground, sitting cross-legged across a red cloth runner, while Abbu's mounting pile of paperwork took up residence on the dining table. Every night after dinner, Abbu would sit hunched over the long immigration forms, making tiny strokes with a black ink pen as he filled out the small boxes, letter by letter, with our personal and financial details. Two years later, we received a letter in the mail saying our application had been accepted. We celebrated by going out for dosas, but none of us finished our meals. By the next day, the dosas had lost their crispiness.

In the summer of 1993, we landed at Pearson International Airport in Toronto, the plane cutting through smoky grey clouds on its descent. Safiya Aunty was waiting for us in the arrivals area, a bouquet of yellow and white roses cradled in the nook of her arm. Her husband, Muneer Uncle, was also there. We were to stay with them until we found a place of our own. As the exit doors parted, a hot, heavy mass of air rushed at us. "This is not how the weather usually is," Muneer Uncle yelled out over the drone of the rushing traffic. By the time we reached their car, the hair at my temples had started to frizz and curl, the humidity reminding me of monsoon season in India when I would put coconut oil in my hair to keep it in place. It didn't occur to me that I might need it here too.

Abbu started looking for work within the first week of our arrival. He visited several employment centres and organizations for newcomers, but had no luck. He had been a professor of commerce at the University of Bombay, but Muneer Uncle told him not to have high hopes. Abbu returned one day looking especially dejected. He sat on the foot of the high king-sized bed and yanked his tie over his head, ruffling his hair.

"It's a maddening thing," he said.

"What is?" Ammi asked.

"This job search. They want you to have Canadian experience. Everything else is irrelevant."

"What happens if you don't find a job?" I asked. Ammi and Abbu turned to look at me, as if they were alarmed by my presence. I had been reading, curled up on an armchair across the room.

"Don't worry about that," Abbu said. "I will find something soon, Insha Allah. What are you reading?"

I held up my book to show him the cover.

"*Jane Eyre*," he said. "They have that here too?"

"I found it at the library. Safiya Aunty took us this morning."

"Good, good." Abbu slowly undid his shirt buttons. "I knew you'd like the libraries here. The Toronto library system is supposed to be one of the best in the world."

"Yes, Abbu," I said, even though I had a feeling he might have just made that up.

"Too bad they don't have libraries like this in India."

"Don't talk so badly about our India," Ammi interjected. "There are good libraries there too." Her head was bent to one side and she was combing her hair, pausing every now and then to untangle the knots with her fingers.

After three weeks of searching, Abbu finally got a job selling newspapers over the phone. He announced the good news over dinner, his voice buoyant. He told us about the lady at the YMCA who helped him apply and prepare for the interview, and how happy she had been when he told her they offered him a position right away. She had three girls too, but they were all grown up, and she lived by herself.

"I felt sad for her. She must feel lonely," Abbu said.

"Kids here usually move out when they go to university. It's good for them, to be on their own and learn how to be independent. Salma will be the first to go," Safiya Aunty said, smiling at me.

"I don't want Aapa to go away," Shaista blurted out, her eyes widening.

"But we came here so we wouldn't have to send the girls away anywhere. So we could be together." Ammi adjusted the dupatta on her head, her bangles clinking softly against each other. Her eyes looked frantic.

"You can't hold them back," Safiya Aunty said, squeezing Ammi's hand.

"But there are universities close by, no?" Ammi looked at Abbu, but he didn't say anything. He dropped a spoonful of tomato chutney onto his plate and massaged it into his rice.

"Different universities are known for different programs," Muneer Uncle explained. "That's why Maria is studying at Queen's University and Abdullah is at the University of Waterloo."

"Do we get to live in dorm rooms, like in the movies?" Aziza asked, her mouth full of food.

Ammi gave her a stern look, then turned back to Safiya Aunty. "Then we will go with them."

"That is all talk for later. Let's figure out where to live first," Abbu finally said, veering the conversation into familiar territory.

Our first home in Canada was a two-bedroom apartment in a low-rise building in Mississauga on Fowler Court, a circular street that had several other buildings on it, all more or less the same height. The unit had been empty and was available for immediate occupancy. It was also close to Abbu's workplace. Abbu, Ammi, and Safiya Aunty took us with them to see the apartment before they signed the lease. The front doors of the building were made of frosted glass; one of the panes had a long crack running down the middle covered with a strip of duct tape. The doors led into a narrow passageway lined with a row of small grey mailboxes on one wall, the unit numbers hand-written on peeling white labels. At the end of the hallway was a single elevator. Our apartment was on the third floor. It smelled like dust and roach spray and I covered my nose with the edge of my shirt sleeve as I walked about with my sisters. The kitchen floor was sticky and the wall above the stove was splattered with orange-brown grease marks. In the bathroom, one of the doors of the cabinet underneath the sink was missing, and in the master bedroom, a large coffee-coloured stain covered about a quarter of the carpet. I thought I would feel relieved when we finally moved into our own home, but walking around the apartment for the first time, I felt more homesick than I had been the past several weeks in Safiya Aunty's house. Even the weather made me long for home. It was hot and humid, making my skin feel grimy, as if all the dust in the apartment had flown up and settled on my body. I was dismayed at the amount of cleaning we would have to do to make the place liveable. I could see even Aziza and Shaista were not impressed, but we all had the sense to say yes when Ammi said to us, "It's nice, isn't it?"

We waited in the car while Abbu, Ammi, and Safiya Aunty went to the landlord's office to sign the lease. When they came out of the building, they stood in the parking lot for a while, Safiya Aunty talking animatedly. The windows were up and the AC was turned on, so I couldn't make out what she was saying. Ammi told us later that night when I asked her about it. The landlord had at first refused to replace the carpet in the master bedroom, saying the bed would cover up the stain, but Safiya Aunty demanded the carpet be replaced or else they would put in a complaint with the city. Ammi told us she was amazed at how Safiya Aunty had spoken so sternly with the landlord and how she wasn't even one bit afraid of him.

"She was right. Why would she be afraid?" Aziza said.

"But he could have done anything to her if he got angry," Ammi said.

"We don't know these people. You might not have been so brave either," I said.

"Oh, please." Aziza rolled her eyes at me. "You're just a scaredy cat."

"Safiya Aunty told us that most people are nice here but you always have to keep an eye out for the bad apples," Ammi said. "But what I didn't understand is, why dishonour the name of a fruit? Why not just say bad people? Why call them bad apples?"

"It's just an expression, Ammi," Aziza said.

"Yes, that much I know too. But I still don't understand it."

The super in our building was not a bad apple. He had a crooked smile, as if the muscles on one side of his face didn't work properly. He waved when he said hello and took his shoes off without being asked. Shaista would watch him intently as he came and went, fixing all the things in the apartment that needed repair.

"Did you see his eyes?" Shaista would come and whisper to us. "They're so blue. Like really, really blue, like the sky."

While the super worked, Ammi put out a tray with a tall glass of orange juice and a saucer with three Danish butter cookies stacked in a crinkly paper cup. But he politely refused the offerings each time, saying, "No, no, not necessary, thank you."

Eventually, I started to feel more settled in our new home. The weather had gotten considerably better as well. The suffocating heatwave had passed and the air smelled of freshly cut grass. I looked forward to Sundays the most when Abbu was off from work and we got to spend the entire day with him. The rest of the week, he worked both the morning and evening shifts and didn't come home until 11:00 pm, his eyes looking puffy, his shoulders slumped from exhaustion. He hardly conversed with us, absent-mindedly leafing through the newspaper as he drank his tea. He seemed withdrawn, like he was a stranger in his own home, and I felt distant from him. But on Sundays, some semblance of normalcy returned and we felt like a family again. After breakfast Abbu would spread out the weekly sale flyers all over the living room carpet and pore through each one, circling the items we needed with a black marker. We would spend the afternoon going to different stores, purchasing a few items from each one. Most of our groceries we bought from Food Basics and Price Chopper. Sometimes we would drive an extra twenty minutes to purchase an item or two from Longo's. It always felt like a treat when we went there. A blast of cool, pine-scented air would greet us as the sliding doors parted. The floor was always shiny and slick, and even the fruits and vegetables looked as if they had been scrubbed and polished before being put out on display. It was at Longo's where Ammi one day picked up a can of pasta sauce and a box of lasagne noodles on sale for 99 cents each. Safiya Aunty had made it for us once and we all liked the way it tasted—like pizza, but saucier and meatier. Ammi decided to try making it for us for dinner one Sunday. I helped her prepare it and warned her when she wasn't following the directions exactly as listed at the back of the box. But Ammi insisted she had to do some things her way, like put turmeric powder and ginger-garlic paste into the ground beef as it cooked. "It will not taste right otherwise," she said, as the meat sat in a lump on the hot frying pan, sparks of muddy water shooting up from its edges. At dinnertime, Aziza set down a knife and fork beside each person's plate, as if we were eating at a restaurant. Ammi brought out the lasagne from the oven, and it looked exactly like Safiya Aunty's—brown and crusty on the edges with streams of red sauce visible under a layer of white cheese. But the sauce tasted funny, tangy and sour, as if some vinegar had been added to it, and the pasta felt hard and gritty in my mouth. It was then that I remembered we had forgotten to boil the lasagne sheets first; there were separate instructions for it on the side of the box, and in our hang-up over how to cook the meat, it must have slipped our minds. We ate silently for a few minutes, knives and forks clanging against our plates.

Shaista spoke up first. "I don't like this," she said, her nose scrunched up.

Ammi blinked quickly, wiping the corner of her eye with the edge of her dupatta. She took our plates, one by one, and with a quick swipe of her hand, dropped the half-eaten squares of lasagne back into the tray and carried it into the kitchen. Later that night, when Ammi was on the phone talking to her sister in Pune, Abbu emptied the lasagne into a plastic bag and threw it down the garbage chute even though it was after 10:00 pm. Then he washed and dried the glass tray and put it away in the drawer under the oven.

About a month later, a notice was slid under our door, informing us that for the next three days, the super and other hired workers would be entering our unit to replace the carpet in the master bedroom. Early the next morning, the super came with two other men, both of whom were tall and muscular with bulging arms and thick necks. One of the men wore a faded white T-shirt with large armholes that looked as if the sleeves had been ripped off. A tattoo peeked out from the back of his T-shirt, a thick ropy vine that extended up and twisted around both sides of his neck, bursting into a cluster of red flower buds just under his ear lobes. As the men worked in the room, scraping and pulling out the original carpet, Shaista stood by the doorway watching them. The super and the other man ignored her, but the man with the tattoo winked at her every now and then, making Shaista giggle. Ammi put out a tray with butter cookies and glasses of orange juice for them, but only the tattooed man drank the juice.

"Mmm. Tastes like curry," he said, smacking his lips.

"Why would he say that?" Ammi muttered after they left. She lifted the juice jug above her head and peered at the markings at the bottom. "Doesn't expire until next week even."

He did the same thing the next day, drinking only the juice and remarking again that it tasted like curry. The other worker smiled or snickered, but I couldn't be sure; his face was shadowed by the bill of his baseball cap. But the super looked down and shook his head slightly, as if exasperated by their behaviour.

On the third day, the men didn't show up early as they had the previous two days. Ammi had a job interview at Food Basics, and she began to get nervous. An hour before she had to leave, there was finally a knock at the door. The men had a giant roll of carpet perched on their shoulders and I held the door open as they awkwardly manoeuvred themselves to come inside.

"Excuse me, but you are very late," Ammi said.

"Yes, sorry, ma'am. We were waiting for the carpet delivery and it was late in coming," the super said.

"I have an important appointment. I need to go out soon." Ammi twirled the edges of her dupatta around her fingers.

"What time?"

"One hour."

The man with the tattoo cleared his throat. "Do you need to go out in one hour? Or go out for an hour?" He spoke loudly and slowly, pausing between each word.

"That is not necessary, Larry," the super said. The other man rotated his baseball cap backwards and chuckled.

"Fucking Pakis," Larry said under his breath. His left hand was balled into a fist, bulging blue-green veins running jaggedly up his arm like river markings on a map.

"What did you say?" Shaista asked. I jumped at the sound of her voice, not realizing she was there.

Larry walked up to her and bent down, placing his large hand over her head and tousling her hair. "I said, fucking Pakis." He reached into his pocket and took out an oval-shaped candy. It was wrapped in a shiny green wrapper that was twisted at the ends like a bow tie.

"But what does it mean?" Shaista asked, taking the candy.

"It means you're all shit." Larry laughed and rubbed her head again. I felt a strange coldness all over, as if someone had opened the door to a freezer and a blast of ice-cold air had gushed into the room. None of us knew what the F-word meant, but we all knew what it meant when someone called you a piece of s-h-i-t. Shaista stood still for a moment, then chucked the candy at Larry. His back was to us, so I don't know if the candy touched any part of him before falling to his feet, but I saw clearly the burst of spit as it landed on her cheek — saw it before I heard him gather the saliva in his mouth with a loud, guttural sound and fling it out on to her face with the sound of a flying kiss.

Ammi let out a scream the same time Shaista's hand smacked her own face. "Chee!" Shaista cried out in disgust, and ran to the bathroom.

"I'm getting the hell out of here," Larry said, his voice low and snarky, laced with anger. It seemed to come at Ammi and me, jumping out at us like the vine poking out from the back of his T-shirt. "Fuck you," he said again before walking out, slamming the door behind him.

The super started to apologize to us, but a loud ringing filled my ears and all I could make out were the sounds of water gushing out of the tap in the bathroom and Shaista's heavy sobs.

Ammi left for her interview a short while later. She instructed me to secure the chain lock that Abbu had installed the day we moved in and told us not to let anyone in while she was gone. Aziza and I tried to play with Shaista but she kept running to the bathroom, rubbing a bar of soap directly on her face. "I can still feel it. It's not gone," she cried, the hefty bar slipping from her tiny hands and falling into the sink with a loud thud.

When Abbu came home that night, Ammi told him what had happened. He walked into our darkened room and knelt by the single twin-sized bed on which we took turns sleeping. He bent down to kiss Shaista's forehead, and she stirred awake. She threw her arms around his neck and started crying again.

"You said we were coming to a kind place, Abbu," Shaista said, her words punctuated with sniffles, "but I don't like it here. I want a kinder home, Abbu."

"Don't cry, beti. We will take care of you. Everything will be okay," Abbu said, rubbing circles on her back. I wanted to go up to him and rest my head on his shoulder, but I stayed huddled against the wall, trying to shake off the gnawing feeling that what had happened was somehow my fault, that I should have never held the door open for them, that I should have spoken instead of Ammi, that I should have been able to save Shaista.

When Ammi woke me up for fajr the next morning, my eyes burned for more sleep, but still I decided to stay up and read Quran. Abbu always said that it was a blessed time when angels came down from the heavens to listen to us recite. The last time I had stayed up after fajr to read Quran was the morning we left India. Everyone else had gone back to sleep after praying, but I had slipped quietly downstairs and settled myself into Abbu's wicker chair. It was where Abbu had sat every afternoon, drinking his chai and reading the newspaper after returning home from work. The newly risen sun had cast a honey-coloured glow over the room and, on the wall in front of me, projected a larger-than-life shadow of the neem tree Abbu had planted on the side of our house. Our living room was empty except for the locked suitcases and taped-up cardboard boxes that stood against the walls. All our furniture had been sold and only the wicker chair remained, the twigs on the back bent and snapped from years of use.

I remembered Abbu's wicker chair again as I dragged a folding chair onto the balcony. I recited Surah Yaseen softly to myself, watching the sky turn from fiery orange to neon pink and eventually dull and dissolve into a clear, cloudless blue. In the parking lot below, black and grey squirrels scampered about, ducking under cars and skittering across wobbly tree branches. I could hear the faint thrumming of a lawn mower in the distance and the consistent chirping of birds, but I couldn't see where they were. Then suddenly a group of small brown sparrows burst out from under a rectangular hedge and dispersed into the sky. I didn't know if they were migratory birds or where they had come from or how long they would stay before leaving. I wondered if birds even had a concept of home, or if home was just a journey, the feeling of wind beneath their wings, criss-crossing oceans and continents in an endless loop.

Later that morning, before Abbu left for work, he went down to the landlord's office to complain about the previous day's events. Abbu returned briefly to inform us that the workers would not be coming back. The super had already told the landlord, and he assured Abbu they would send new workers to finish the job. Abbu surprised us that night by coming home an hour early and taking us out to McDonalds. We each bought our own soft-serve ice cream cone, finishing it in the car on the way home.

The next day, Ammi got a phone call from Food Basics. She got the job she had interviewed for and they wanted her to start immediately. Ammi was hesitant, but I pushed her to go and reassured her that we would be all right. She told us repeatedly not to open the door for anyone and to secure the chain lock as soon as we closed the door behind her. After she left we watched *The Price is Right* and played a couple of rounds of UNO before getting ready for duhr. For lunch, I reheated the leftovers from last night's dinner. We ate in silence, feeling strange and awkward to be eating a meal by ourselves. Ammi and Abbu had left us alone only a handful of times before, like when they went to visit Ammi's family in Pune and Aziza and I had exams to study for. They would leave all three of us behind and ask our neighbour, Khadija Aunty, to check in on us. She would come knocking at lunchtime, carrying a large steel platter, with bowls of curry covered with turned up saucers and a heaping tray of rice. An hour later, she would return to trade the empty dishes for a plate of sliced mangoes or guavas. But there was no one here to check up on us, and we passed the rest of the time after lunch reading books we had borrowed from the library.

Ammi returned at 3:00 pm in a pair of black pants and a dark-green collared T-shirt.

"Is that a uniform? Do you have to wear that?" Aziza asked, examining her from top to bottom.

"Yes." Ammi stood up taller. "Do you like it?"

"No."

Ammi sighed. "I don't like it either. But at least it's a job, and the manager is a very nice man." Ammi told us he too was an immigrant and had come here from Jamaica eighteen years before. "I can't imagine being here for almost twenty years," Ammi said. "Sometimes I can't even believe we're not in India anymore."

Ammi woke me up early the next morning so she could give me instructions on how to cook chicken curry for lunch. She had cut up a whole chicken the night before and left it in a mixing bowl in the fridge, marinating in a spiced yogurt mixture. Before she left, she took the bowl out of the fridge and placed it on the counter so the chicken could return to room temperature. It was another humid day; the air felt heavy and smelled like rotting apples. We left the windows and balcony open all the way, but there was not even the slightest breeze to cool us. Even my eyelids felt sticky. I stretched myself out on the sofa and was just starting to drift off to sleep when I heard a loud knock on the door. My eyes flew open and I stayed very still. There was a short pause, followed by another, louder knock. I sat up, my heart beating rapidly, and willed myself to get up and look through the peephole.

A man with small, beady eyes and greying hair had his face right up to the door. "Hello?" he called out in a gruff voice.

I jumped back from the door.

He knocked again, harder. "Hello?"

"Who is it?" My voice came out croaky and raspy, and I had to clear my throat and repeat myself.

"Landlord. I need to check something."

I spoke into the sliver of space between the edge of the door and the door frame. "Can you come back, please, sir?"

"I need to check something. I was just about to let myself in."

I heard keys jingle behind the door. "Come back, please. At three o'clock," I called out again. My mouth felt dry and pasty, and my heart rammed against the walls of my chest. I looked through the peephole again. The man was staring right at me. He had deep lines around his mouth and a dimple in his chin that looked like a scar.

"I'm busy later. I just need to check something, okay? I'm going to let myself in."

All sorts of vicious thoughts ran through my mind. What if he wasn't the landlord? What if Larry, the man with the tattoo, was standing right next to him, just outside my view, carrying a gun or a knife? I took a step backwards, expecting the door to swing open. The muggy scent of raw chicken filled my nostrils and I was struck by a sudden fear that the meat had started to spoil. I turned my head towards the kitchen, and something I hadn't noticed before caught my eye. On the side of the fridge, hidden halfway behind the kitchen wall, was a notepad-sized magnet with a list of emergency numbers. On the top, in bright red, was 911. I suddenly remembered the chain lock on the door and reached up and held it taut.

"No," I said loudly. "My parents said come back at three o'clock, please."

"I told you I am busy. I need to come in now."

"Please leave, or I will call the police," I blurted out. "I will call the police and I will tell them someone is trying to come into our home when my parents are not here." I could hardly believe what I was saying, but I kept my voice steady, continuing to hold on to the chain lock so tightly I was afraid it might snap.

The door shook with a loud thud, and I pressed my shoulder up against it. "I'm going to call the police if you don't leave," I said again, louder.

"Okay, okay, okay."

I looked through the peephole and saw him back away from the door and then disappear, his heavy footsteps echoing down the hallway. I let go of the chain lock, its criss-cross pattern imprinted into the fleshy parts of my fingers, and slid down to the floor. My face felt hot, like someone had been holding a flame to my cheeks. I forced myself to take long, slow breaths and rubbed my sweaty palms on my pants. When I felt my composure return, I went to our room. The floor fan whirred noisily, giving both Aziza and Shaista a prolonged blast of air as its face swept across the room. It was Aziza's turn to sleep on the bed and she was lying on her stomach, her pyjama pants bunched up around her knees, exposing the mounds of her fleshy calves. Shaista was on the ground, lying on her back with her hands folded atop her chest, sleeping in the same way that Abbu slept. I felt my throat closing in and tears gathering in my eyes. I remembered Khadija Aunty again: her rosewater smell and her tight, rib-crushing hugs. Aziza used to complain that she hugged someone as if she would never see them again. The day we left India, she had stood in the middle of our street, her nose and eyes red from crying, waving her arm high in the air. I watched her get smaller and smaller from the rear window of our taxi until we rounded the corner, and I knew then that I would never see her again.

Ammi had told me to wake up Aziza so she could help me cook, but I closed the door with a soft click and went into the kitchen. I peeled back the plastic film that covered the bowl of chicken, careful not to let the water that had condensed on its underside drip onto the floor. I bent my head over the bowl and sniffed. I couldn't detect the muggy scent that had hit me earlier, just the tanginess of the yogurt and the burn of pepper.

The new carpet for Ammi and Abbu's bedroom stood propped up against the wall in our living room for more than a week before the super returned with two new men to finish the job. Abbu took the day off work and stayed in the living room reading the previous night's paper. Ammi went to work, and no one served the men butter cookies or orange juice. They came and left without incident and in a matter of a few hours, Ammi and Abbu's bedroom had a brand new carpet, rose pink with plush fibres that made light and dark patterns when we dragged our feet all over it. The next summer, when our lease was due to expire, we moved into a new apartment in a high-rise building close to Square One. The hallways were brightly lit and covered with a textured sea-green wallpaper. In our apartment, all the kitchen appliances were brand new, including the tap, from which water came out in a single gush or, with the push of a black rubber button, in multiple streams like a showerhead. The building management had their cleaners come into the unit before we moved in, and all the necessary repairs were taken care of as well. "If we missed anything, just give me a call," the super told us, sticking a magnetic business card on the fridge door. He spoke with a European accent — maybe Spanish or Italian, I couldn't tell for sure — and he had a very red face and breathed heavily, as if he had run some long distance just a few minutes before, as if he had journeyed all the way there from Spain or Italy and hadn't had time to recover or catch his breath just yet. "Welcome to the neighbourhood," he said, and left us to unload our furniture and arrange our new home.

ARMAGEDDON BY TARANTINO

Graham Robert Scott

Graham Robert Scott *resides in Texas, grew up in California, and owns neither cowboy hat nor surfboard. When he isn't teaching as an English professor at Texas Woman's University, he writes fiction, with stories appearing in* Orca, X-R-A-Y, Nature, *and elsewhere. His story 'A Parable of Things that Crawl and Fly', co-written with Wallace Cleaves, appears in* Pulp Literature *Issue 25, Winter 2020.*

© 2021, Graham Robert Scott

Armageddon by Tarantino

Ellie misses the football, not because she's eight but because she's staring at the sky.

This is how I know another star's exploded.

I rush to block her view of the heavens, and, finger to chin, nudge her gaze back to Earth.

"You all right?" I ask.

She nods. I watch her chest as her breathing returns to normal.

Everyone else ignores the star. Mom *mise-en-places* the dinner line. Cousins toss bean bags and Frisbees. Bruce sits by the radio, even though it's off, even though there's no game on, because as far as he's concerned there should be a game.

We have Chamberlain Park to ourselves today. No one else is on the grass.

The emptiness everywhere I go feels like a drumbeat, a message. When I showed up for Astronomy yesterday, I found row upon row of vacant seats facing an untended lectern. Crowds can be found in obvious places, of course. At the grocery store, the lines go all the way to the milk.

But here, at the park, it's just us.

In every hurricane, there's some idiot family that refuses to evacuate.

Ellie glances at the sky again.

"Nothing's hit us," I say.

Ellie nods. She's become so quiet lately that I gauge her mood from the vigour of her head movements. Shallow and hesitant, I think, means *not yet*. If so, she isn't wrong. Every few hours a star in our sky explodes, but with all the energy channelled into beams, like water jets from a hose with a thumb over the opening. Been going like that a few days now. No one knows why.

So far we're just getting droplets from the side. Nothing straight on, not yet, or we'd be toast.

Ellie taps the phone in my pocket and gazes a question.

"Okay," I say.

Side by side in the grass, we scroll news on my phone.

"Don't go freaking her out," Mom calls, knifing king's cake into wedges. What she means is *don't watch the news*. And what that means is that Bruce has become Mom's barometer for truth. Which I knew. As a younger woman, she'd homeschooled us through the pandemic that killed Dad. When I look at her, I still see the woman who woke me after midnight to spy on Saturn's rings through a telescope. Mom continues, "Ellie had nightmares last night."

Yes, I think. *I was the one who dealt with them.*

My phone chirps. It's Zoe, the only Burroughs missing, disinvited after her accusations. Her text reads, *Is he there?*

"Is who here?" Ellie asks, as Bruce pops the tab on another beer.

Yeah, I reply. *I'm with Ellie.*

Ellie gives me a quizzical look.

"She worries about you," I say.

"Because of the stars?"

"Just generally. It's a big-sister thing."

Last night, when Ellie dreamed of angry stars, it was Zoe she cried for. But since Zoe's with friends now, Mom sent up Bruce. Who shouldn't have been over in the first place. Who shouldn't now be in the park with us. But who knows the sheriff. So.

I cut him off at Ellie's door. "I've got it," I said. Repeated it, as Bruce lurked in the doorway, blotted against the hall light. After he skulked away, I held Ellie's hand as her breathing steadied and her eyes closed.

Ellie taps my phone: a video of my professor on the newsfeed.

"Oh, I saw that one," I say. This is true. I watched it last night on earbuds while I held Ellie's hand. "It wasn't very good." This is untrue, but the video will do nothing to ease her mind.

"Looks like star wars to me." The interviewer didn't mean the movie.

My professor sighed. "But it can't——"

Downstairs, sounds of Bruce rummaging in the kitchen. Fridge opening, the clink of a bottle, fridge closing.

"Why not?"

"Okay. Here's a star that blew up a thousand years ago. Here's one that blew up sixty years back. They're not even close to happening at the same time. But because of the different distances, the light from all the detonations reaches us within hours of each other. The only place this all looks synchronous——stars being fired at each other, Armageddon directed by Tarantino——is Earth."

"What's your explanation, then?"

"Don't have one."

"Nothing?"

New sounds. TV clicking on. Cialis ad.

The professor paused. "Maybe it's a long, long war, and the way it looks to us, all simultaneous, is a coincidence." He sounded unconvinced.

"We're back to war."

"Or it's some phenomenon we don't understand."

"Tautology."

"Or …"

"What?"

"A message. Stars aimed at each other, but the message aimed at us."

"A message."

"Yeah."

Downstairs, a belch.

"And the message?"

"Don't fuck with us. We have stars to burn."

Ellie runs around the grass and Buster Keatons the football.

Mom explains we need more ice. Would I be a dear?

I hesitate.

The ball rolls to my feet. Ellie gestures.

Mom hands me a ten. "Bruce can watch her."

"No."

Mom scowls. "She'll be fine. Zoe's being a drama queen. Women's studies poisoned that girl's brain."

Bruce calls Ellie, pats the bench beside him.

I grab the ball, cry *look sharp,* and spiral it past her shoulder.

Ellie turns —

— the sky brightens —

—and the world gleams white.

Ellie cries out, hands over her face.

Closing the distance, I scoop Ellie against my shoulder. Then I'm running, throwing legs ahead of me for every inch I can gain.

"I've got you," I say as she clutches my shirt.

Behind us, shouts and confusion. A cousin yells it's a false alarm.

The Sun, emerging from behind the clouds.

But now that I'm running, I can't stop. It's like crying once the tears start.

On McKinley, just off the park, a man tapes Hefty bags to his windows. A woman and a tween port canned goods indoors from a truck. They pause as I huff by, Ellie now sobbing, and I can see the question in their eyes. *Don't you have a place to be?*

THE SEARCH

Colleen Anderson

Colleen Anderson's writing has appeared in numerous fiction and poetry venues, such as Nevermore, Beauty of Death, Amazing, OnSpec, Heroic Fantasy Quarterly, and Cemetery Dance. A three-time Aurora nominee, she has received honourable mentions for poetry and fiction. Her past roles include book buyer, book rep, poetry editor, reading series host, anthology editor, and freelance copy editor. Colleen has received Canada Council and BC Arts Council grants for writing, and was nominated for a Pushcart Prize. Black Shuck Books published her dark fiction collection A Body of Work. Find her at colleenanderson.wordpress.com.

© 2021, Colleen Anderson

The Search

The droning of summer thrummed the day with expectation. Pine trees poked at the sky, lessening the sun's glare. In the lake's placid, deep blue depths, hidden things moved. The water humped, a darker shade growing, and Tanis stood, her breath contained. The shape didn't breach, dissipating into shadows and mystery. She waited, hoping.

Tanis sighed, sitting again on the bench, the liquorice and orange of her ice cream cone tingling her tongue. Her attention followed the ancient stone hills rolling up on either side of the valley, which had long ago become a natural reservoir. The full, heavy air had been waiting for a thousand years with the patience that only nature can endure. Had it always been this way, knowing secrets and waiting for others to discover them?

She stared at the glassy water and thought that shadow, *there*, might be the lake monster, but she knew better. Ogopogo's elusive trail wound through Okanagan Lake's long, deep trench. She would wait forever if she needed to. She rubbed at her eyes and sighed.

"What are you doing?"

A boy stood to her right, lanky, in tattered shorts and a striped shirt, maybe a year or two older and more interested in her ice cream cone than the lake.

"I'm searching for N'ha-a-itk." She stumbled over the unfamiliar word, so it came out as *naa ah teek*.

He scratched his head, hair a dark brown tousle, and squinted at her. His worn sandals were in his other hand as he worked his toes into the pebbled sand of Peachland's narrow beach. "What's that?"

"You know." She pointed to a picture in one of her books—a smiling green serpent with horns. "Ogopogo, but that's not its real name."

The boy scrunched up his face and rolled his eyes. He seemed torn between letting the lures of summer pull him in another direction and learning more. He looked out at the water and back to her books.

For a moment, she couldn't say anything, licking furiously to keep the ice cream from dripping onto her books. The sun itched her skin, and her legs had an inner shiver that almost hurt. If she watched long enough she'd see the lake monster, no matter how many years it might take. Eventually . . .

Tanis peered at him. "The Okanagan people named it N'ha-a-itk and used to give it live sacrifices so they could row safely across the lake."

"There's no such thing as monsters." He stood and moved away. "Besides, feeding living things to something is disgusting."

She thought about that. It might have been difficult to throw a live animal into the lake. "But how do you know Ogopogo is not real?"

"I just do." He waved to her as the beach succeeded in pulling him along.

"I'm Tanis," she yelled after him. He was probably going back to Kelowna, so she should have said goodbye.

"James" wafted back to her as gulls cried overhead.

Summer hung on hard that year, reluctant to let the winter in. Gradually the fall crept through the trees, painting them tangerine and russet. Tanis pedalled her bike out to the beach every chance she had. She always chose the spot closest to Squally Point, which had the most reported sightings. The day coated her in warmth, but her mother had made her pack her thick green sweater, along with a snack and a needless admonition not to go swimming by herself in the lake.

She sat on a tan log abandoned on the beach. Calling the water 'waves' would have been a boast for the water. The ripples pushed at the shore gently, as if from a bowl tilted back and forth. What secrets did it conceal under the calm surface? Tanis had pleaded with her parents to take her out in a motorboat, but they didn't see the point.

Someday when she was older, she would rent a boat and search as far as she could.

"You're wasting your time, you know."

She looked up, pushing hair out of her face. His jeans and denim shirt draped him loosely, as if he'd stolen an older brother's clothes.

"You're not going swimming?"

James shook his head. "Too chilly." He glanced at her and put his hands on his hips, staring at the lake as if he could conquer it with a glance. "Not that I would mind, but I have to go to the store. We're just here another few days, then back to Kelowna."

He toed one of the books beside her. "They just want to make money. It's all a tourist thing."

She tilted her head. Her mom and dad said the same thing, and she wondered if he was just saying what his parents told him. Yet her parents watched enough TV shows that weren't real, so what did it matter? "Not all of it is. Some people were really scared when they saw the serpent of the lake."

James grunted and crossed his arms. "Just actors."

"Then what about the people from a hundred years ago? They weren't acting or bringing in tourists. It was part of their legends."

Reaching for a stick in the sand, James grabbed it and poked it around. "People didn't know as much then. A log in the water, some storm, whatever; they just made up stories to entertain themselves because they didn't know the truth."

She thought she saw something and stood, facing the point. A dark shape in the distance clouded the water's surface. James laughed beside her.

"We know the truth. See?" He pointed up. "That cloud casts shadows on the water."

Everyone laughed at her for hunting Ogopogo, but she just knew it was real. "I can see that, but I have to check because someday, maybe, it will appear." She glanced at him, annoyed by the way he acted as if he knew everything. "Maybe I should give it a sacrifice."

"What?" He turned to her, anger lancing his eyes. "Are you nuts? What are you going to do — buy a hamster and toss it into the water to drown, or find some hamburger to throw in the lake?"

"I—I wasn't going to kill anything. Geez. It was a joke."

"It's stupid to think of this stuff." James continued to lunge as if he were attacking the lake.

Tanis dug her nail into the log and spoke slowly. "Don't you think it would be amazing to find something … different? To find out that a myth was real? You can still believe in Ogopogo. I do."

He laughed, the sound lacking any joy. Taking the thick stick, James jumped up and stalked up and down the beach. "If — *if* — there was such a monster, you know what I would do? I would be like St George and the dragon. I would hunt it down because it held people hostage by making them give sacrifices. That's what the dragon did too. It was a bully. It scared them. And if I could find it, I would skewer it and slice off its head." He stabbed the air with his stick, swishing it left and right. "Now *that* would bring in the tourists and stop these lame stories."

Tanis jumped up. "That's horrible!" Crying, she threw her books in her bag and jumped on her bike. "I hate you!" She pedalled away before James could catch up.

His voice sounded like a gull's as she sped away from the lake. "It's only make-believe!"

In three years, puberty caught up to her, as well as other changes that moved through her in small tremors. But her need to encounter N'ha-a-itk, to meet a creature of myth, pulled at her stronger than before. An ache sometimes seized her legs, leaving them throbbing and too tender to walk.

Something weaved Tanis's thoughts to the lake; the myth and mystery burned bright and hot as if she held a sun within her heart. She imagined herself the warrior protector of the ancient lake. The trees, the beach, and the small wildflowers were the fortress surrounding it. *This* was her home, and she loved it here.

She had exhausted all the available reading material, though she kept a few well-thumbed books and searched the internet regularly, expanding her knowledge to include the plants and animals that seeded the land around Okanagan Lake. While other kids were following gossip sites, liking pages, downloading fantasy novels, and reading up on various bands, Tanis continued to read about the local trees and flowers, and the wildlife.

She walked along the beachfront, noting flotsam that washed up onshore, and peered occasionally through her binoculars. A figure that looked vaguely familiar walked toward her. She pulled out her earbuds, trading the song for the susurrus of trees and grass. A motorboat droned in the distance, and the water softly slapped the shore. Squatting, she punctured the water's surface with her fingers and sent a voiceless plea to Ogopogo. Her fingers tingled and warmed.

"What are you doing?"

She stayed that way a moment longer, sighing when nothing came of it. As she stood, Tanis looked at James. He had grown taller. His voice crackled between high and low, as if coming over a bad radio station.

"You're not still mad at me, are you?" He seemed to really want to know, a touch of worry creasing his brows.

Tanis looked out at the lake. "Not really, but that all depends on what you say, now, doesn't it?"

He smiled and shrugged. "Well, my opinion hasn't changed."

"Neither has mine." Tanis started walking again, leaving it up to him whether to follow. She felt more than saw him beside her. "Do you always make fun of other people's beliefs?"

She glanced at him as he stared at the ground, kicking twigs and stones along.

"I don't … always. It's just that I can't understand why anyone would waste their time chasing ghosts and monsters. Why do you want to find Ogopogo?"

Watching her runners flash white as she walked, she gave it thought. How could she explain the need that burned stronger every year, the yearning that tugged her soul? "I just want to know there is more to the world."

A plaintive tone laced James's voice. "But why? What would that mean?"

She used her binoculars to investigate several dark blobs, but they were only bobbing logs, mocking her. "It would mean there is magic, that anything might be possible."

James shook his head. He picked up a few rocks and skipped them over the lake's skin. "I don't get it. There is so much in this world. People have created art, buildings, planes … gone to the moon, even. Isn't that magic enough?"

"Not for me." Tanis bent down again and scooped a few pebbles from the water's edge: brown, grey, flecked, a reddish stone or two. They held no mystery, but as she let them trickle through her fingers, it felt as if a hot poker had been jammed up her legs. She fell, bruising her butt on the rocky beach.

"Ow, ow, ow."

James's voice came muffled as she rocked back and forth, rubbing her legs, trying to ease the fiery lightning coursing through them. "Hey, you okay?"

His hand weighted her shoulder and stopped her rocking. Fire seared her. She took several deep breaths, the pain blurring away, the lake's quiet murmur soothing her. She grunted. "Yeah, I think so. Just some weird pain." There had been twinges before but nothing like this. She tried to hide the twitching down her legs.

He helped her stand.

"I think I'd better go. I'll see you sometime in the summer, I guess."

James shrugged. "Probably. Hope school doesn't suck."

The lake always called, even when the mysterious razor wire of agony wrapped her lower limbs. The doctors couldn't pinpoint it, said it was some phenomenon of growing pains. Still, when the ghost ache wasn't crippling her, Tanis walked the shoreline, always searching for the elusive N'ha-a-itk. She took a cane now to keep her from falling whenever the pain unexpectedly grabbed her.

After her sixteenth birthday, she ventured further with the scooter she had bought. In the more secluded spots she dove into the water, its cool balm the only thing that seemed to assuage the pain. Tanis rowed out into the lake to use her snorkel and underwater camera, but sometimes she abandoned it all to dive into the depths, sending thoughts out to N'ha-a-itk.

No matter where on the long lake she wandered, she felt the pull, but she never saw anything. Tanis loved the water, and it gave her some comfort when she submerged herself.

The ache that rippled through her limbs had never gone away, though now it grew subtler, a ghost of its initial onslaught. The cane was tucked away but always near. Just as she knew that N'ha-a-itk existed, so she knew she would run into James again, though it didn't happen until she enrolled at the Kelowna campus.

"Hey, Tanis!"

She smiled at James, now fully six feet, his hair only slightly longer but still neat.

"How goes it?"

"It goes," she said. "What are you studying?"

He grinned. "Well, I think I'll go into law, but I have this first year to truly decide. What about you? Still hunting lake monsters?"

"Perhaps, but right now I have to get to class. Environmental studies."

"'Kay. Let's catch up. Meet me at the front steps at seven for dinner. I'm buying."

He waved and walked away before she answered.

They didn't often discuss Tanis's 'obsession', as James called it, with Okanagan Lake. When they did, the void between them widened, with Tanis retreating to her books and James to beer with his buddies.

She continued to drive home every weekend she could, with an inevitable swim or boat trip onto the lake.

She and James had taken a motorboat out to Squally Point and climbed the rough rock. James complained about the lack of grass and the shifting rocks. Tanis loved to seek purchase in the cracks and crevices, as if she were a plant trying to take root. There were small mauve and white flowers and tufts of moss that softened the stone face.

They lay side by side, letting the heat massage them. Tanis's legs were nearly as brown as James's from all her time outside. The field trips for her assignments made her studies more wonderful.

Sleepily, he asked, "Are you still searching?"

"Always. But it's more complex now." She sat up, sweeping her hand toward the lake. "The Westbank First Nation considers N'ha-a-itk to be a metaphor. It is the spirit that resides in the water but can also be part of the land and the air."

James scowled briefly, then looked pensive, rolling to his side and asking her, "So you no longer think Ogopogo is real?"

She pulled a tuft of bunchgrass, slowly peeling it into strips. "I didn't say that. I hope someday that I will encounter N'ha-a-itk, but in the meantime, I'll consider it the spirit of the lake. The Westbank Nation says that if N'ha-a-itk disappears, so too will the plants, trees, and food that sustain us all. And that's why I'm in environmental science, because if pollution takes all that away, then N'ha-a-itk will truly be extinct."

James sat up. "I can understand that, but if it's just a metaphor, then is it needed at all? Conservation can always be carried out without relying on myth."

As the first year drew to a close, Tanis waited eagerly to spend more time on the water and in it, embracing N'ha-a-itk in her own way. She was sitting near Squally Point, where a road came close enough for an easy hike along the mountainous cliff. Gazing over the lake, a deep, contented peace filled her.

James sat down beside her. They were shifting onto different planes, unable to keep their tenuous hold on the same belief system.

"Thought I'd find you here."

"Hmm." His warmth cooled her right side as he sat beside her.

"Look, finals are in a few weeks, and I wanted to talk to you about something."

She looked over to him but didn't say anything.

"I've decided I will go into law, but I need to move to Vancouver. I was wondering what you were thinking. You could continue your studies there."

She smiled at him and ran a finger along his lovely jaw. "I can't leave the lake. It's my lifeblood. The environment I'm specializing in is this area."

James's mouth turned down. "But we have a good thing going. You would still be able to specialize."

"I'm sorry, but I can't." She stood, putting her pack on. She looked down at her conflicted lover. "Tell me. Do you remember long ago when you said you would kill the Ogopogo if you ever saw it?"

"I was a kid. I had my fantasies, just as you did. But what does this have to do with moving to Vancouver?"

She pulled back her hair and buttoned her jacket. The sun had nearly sunk behind the hills, and James became a shadow against the lake's darker silhouette. "Just suppose for a minute that definitive proof of the Ogopogo, or ghosts, or Sasquatch, existed. Would you still want to see them killed?"

The last light of day glinted sharply in his eyes. His face closed, and she could no longer read him.

"Well, would you?"

He replied gruffly. "I wouldn't, but I would want to see them gone. There is no place for outmoded mythologies. This is our world now. People waste too much time on history. We need to live in the present, and so do you."

She turned from him, even though the lake called to her. "Then I wish you the best with your career. I'll be staying here."

Her legs burned and twitched, and she bit her lip to keep from crying out. Stripping down in the dusk, not worried about anyone seeing her on a Tuesday night, she dove into the bracing waters of Okanagan Lake.

The water stroked her legs, and she would have sighed if

liquid didn't surround her. The cool caress eased the burning and elongated her limbs. The black viscosity of the night-painted water buoyed her, pulling her into its waves. Tanis floated, feeling the spasms in her limbs dissipate and the long heartbroken ache in her soul dissolve. Her neck stretched; her body swelled. The water grew warm against her thickened skin. She rolled, ecstatic, filled with a lifting wonder. As her flippers cleaved the lake, she dove deep, sounding in the depths. A vibration hummed in her that indicated the shoreline where the thickest trees were, areas that felt cold and dead. Sickness lurked there.

She did not need to breach the surface as she caught and ate a trout. It tasted fresh, crisp, a bit like parsley and smoke. Tanis was a mosaic of the lake, the shoreline, the weeds that grew in the water, the other creatures that lived there. She understood, now, why there had never been definitive proof. N'ha-a-itk had to be protected. The night belonged to Tanis, and she swam the length of the lake. Only as she moved toward the shore, her flippers shrinking back into digits, her body becoming small and human, did she move above the waterline.

Her chest felt full, weighted with a deep subtleness that completed her, making her whole for the first time since she had started her search. The pain in her limbs disappeared. For a time she sat on the rocks and cried, mingling her salt tears with the cool lake water.

BEHIND THE SUMACS

Samuel Strathman

Samuel Strathman *is a poet, visual artist, author, and kitchen coordinator. He is also the founder/editor-in-chief of Floodlight Editions. His debut poetry collection* Omnishambles *is forthcoming with Ice Floe Press.*

© 2021, Samuel Strathman

Behind the Sumacs

During a grocery
run, a hawk draws
forward like a velvet
curtain,
kidnapping a

squirrel in the

process.

Her feet never
touch the ground
as she spools back
with her prize,

vanishing before the
dust can settle. Perhaps
she's afraid
that I'm what jackrabbits

behind the sumacs.
Perhaps I am,
but now my brain
needs oxygen
so it can rewire

to its chassis. The first
features to twitch
are my face muscles
—nosebleed,
dyspnea,

mirroring my surroundings.

IT WAS A CHUPI AFTER ALL

Elsa M Carruthers

Elsa M Carruthers *is a speculative fiction writer, academic, and poet. She earned an MFA in Writing Popular Fiction from Seton Hill University. Since graduating, Elsa's fiction and poetry have been published in several anthologies, magazines, and e-zines. Some of her academic work is published in* Uncovering Stranger Things: Essays on Nostalgia, Cynicism, and Innocence in the Series; The Streaming of Hill House; *and* The Many Lives of The Twilight Zone. *She lives in California with her family.*

© 2021, Elsa M Carruthers

$\mathcal{I}$T Was a Chupi After All

We picked the Lucky's parking lot, figuring it would be full and at least one driver would leave the gas cap unlocked. I had the hose and bucket in hand, already thinking this was going to land our sorry asses in juvie, when Rogelio stopped and, pointing to a run-down Buick, shouted, "This one, Hector!"

My heart beat hard in my chest and I felt a cramp forming. I swivelled my head around to make sure we weren't heard — or worse, spotted.

"Quit making so much noise, *pendejo!*" I said to Rogelio. He kept singing Banda Machos's 'La Culebra' and doing a stupid shuffle step.

"Oooh, *hay viene el Chupacabra,*" he said to me in a haunted voice.

"Just shut up or I'll *show* you a chupi!"

The mysterious creature was all anyone was talking about. When I had been getting ready that morning, the song on the radio was interrupted by another news flash:

As another wave of strange animal sightings and pet casualties goes through the city and outlying areas of Bakersfield, local authorities are urging residents to keep garbage cans away from houses to discourage animals from scavenging near homes and attacking pets.

While the animal or animals remain unidentified and uncaptured, animal control reminds everyone to stay calm, keep pets indoors, and refrain from engaging with wild animals . . .

Rogelio kept saying, "Chup-aaa . . . caa-braaa," in a soft, singsong voice.

"*Idiota*," I mumbled as I set the bucket down and unrolled the garden hose we'd cut. I had half a mind to sock him one, but that would just slow us down. Besides, I wanted to be done and out of there. Rogelio was in an invincible mood, and there was no talking sense to him when he was like that.

He already had the cap off and had snaked one end of the hose into the tank. He crouched next to me, the other end of the hose already in his mouth. His lean cheeks pulled in as he created suction.

I stared off toward the other end of the parking lot and saw something scuttle. It moved too strangely to be a dog, though it was the right size. It seemed to be hunting something, the way it hunched in the shadows. I struggled to get a good look.

The splash and smell of gasoline called my attention back. Rogelio left enough gas for the person to get home (we never left people stranded—that would get us caught) and moved on to a newer Chevy sedan. I had to jimmy the cap free, but moments later Rogelio was sucking the gas out of that tank too.

We heard the metallic scrape of a shopping cart on asphalt. Time to go. I hustled the best I could without splashing gas all over the place, and Rogelio dragged the hose on the ground as he hoofed it out of there, leaving me behind.

When I finally got to Angel's place, a 900-square-foot, newly plastered house with black scrolled-iron security bars on every window, fucking Rogelio was outside, trying to shoot the shit with one of Angel's men. The guy stood there sneering, his muscle shirt and Dickies pressed into hard creases, thick gold ropes around his bulldog neck.

I noted the heavy prison tats. The intricate lettering and dark pigmentation told me they were all done outside the US. I lifted my chin to him in respect and made like the bucket was nothing to carry.

Fuck that noise too, 'cause it was heavy as all get-out. It had been my stupid idea to use a plastic paint pail. I couldn't slide it on the handlebars of my bike without the damned handle snapping and breaking. So there I was, like a *pinche pendejo*, hauling it around by hand.

"*¿Que onda?*" Bulldog dude asked me before he turned to Rogelio. He told Rogelio that it was bullshit to leave me to carry the bucket more than two blocks by myself. I liked the guy immediately.

Rogelio's cheeks went pale and he mumbled something. I was waiting for the go-ahead to put the pail down and get our pay. Angel would have his people get the gas to those who needed it.

Dude wasn't done with Rogelio, though.

It wasn't that Rogelio was selfish or anything. He was a giant kid. His mind went crazy with ideas, and he just couldn't think of stuff like logistics. I think he's a little slow too, but I'd never tell him that. He's my best friend.

I set the pail down and rubbed my arm. I needed to go home to my family. I waved and started on my way, and called out that Angel could pay me later. Rogelio tagged behind me. I didn't even slow my stride.

"You heard what he said, right?" I asked him. Rogelio huffed and fell into step with me as we turned the block to my street, a cul-de-sac of tiny, brightly painted houses with people spilling onto postage-stamp yards and the permanent smells of beans, rice, tortillas, and engine oil in the air. There is always a radio or two blasting Cumbias, or ranchera music to drown out someone's family drama.

"*Animal World* is going to do a special here about the animal control thing." Rogelio pulled an entertainment magazine from his back pocket and opened it to the article. His face glowed with excitement.

"Why do we care? It's not like we're getting paid or will even be in it." I was still annoyed at him, but I glanced at the open page.

ANIMAL WORLD TO SHOOT IN CALIFORNIA TOWN
Michael Korsec gives the green light for a new show centred around wild animals in urban areas. The pilot, which focuses on how raccoons have adapted to Chicago, is already in production. Animal World will air in the fall.

"See?" he said.

"Yeah. Gotta go."

My *abuelos* were waiting for me on the tiny porch. My *abuela*, Rosa, had the newspaper in hand, ready for me to read it to them. This had to be done every day, and in the exact way they wanted. My *abuelo*, Roberto, had circled the articles for me to read. They didn't even let me get a cup of water; I was late, and they wanted me to start.

With a sigh, I read the first one in English so they could get a feel for the words, and then translated it to help them understand. In this way, they'd been learning English at a good clip.

The first circled article was a small story about a new store going in, and my abuelos nodded as if it were the most important thing to ever happen. But I knew they wanted the animal story, with all the pictures of the county animal control vans. I saved it for last because it was super long and because that was the way they liked it.

Even at church, the buzz was all chupi, all the time, and the older folks couldn't get enough. They conversed amongst themselves and warned us to keep *ojos pelados*. But it was the best thing that had ever happened to me and Rogelio as far as girls went.

I had a steady rotation of dates with Miranda and Nina, and I was chatting up Blanca too. Even Rogelio was suddenly on the radar. Lupita was practically glued to him lately.

I started the article. My abuelos were convinced it was a Chupacabra, no matter how many times I tried to tell them otherwise.

"El Chupacabra, *otra vez en la ciudad*," Abuela said with excitement. She thinks our city has a Chupacabra and that it is lonely, looking for a mate. "*Ojalá*," she started, but my abuelo cut her off by putting his hand on hers. He wanted me to read; he was way more invested in this story than he wanted to admit.

I quickly told them about *Animal World*, and Abuela gave us both a satisfied smile.

The headline read, Local Animal Control Officer Loses Finger, and for the first time, even I was into it. The story recapped the other sightings of a stray animal, possibly a coyote. "*No es coyote*," Abuelo interrupted.

"Okay, Abuelo," I said. Already my mind was connecting the thing in the parking lot and the thing that bit some poor *payaso's* finger clean off before making a break for it.

They almost caught the animal with one of those poles with a metal hoop on the end, but the officer, whose name was withheld, was by himself. From his hospital bed, he told reporters that he wasn't supposed to capture the animal without calling it in first. He was ordered to engage. I knew he was telling the truth, and he would make serious bank when he sued the county.

"*Sí pues, obvio que lo mandaron a la* Chupacabra *solito. El pobre,*" my abuela said. It was obvious to her that the guy was made to face the Chupacabra by himself.

A Kern County animal control officer was hospitalized after an animal attack. An investigation is underway. Sources suggest that an increase in illegal exotic animal hoarding and breeding may be responsible.

Numerous reports have been called in for sightings of an unidentified creature lurking in parking lots, shopping centres, and alleys. More disturbing, several of the reports made mention of pet dogs mating with the mysterious creature.

To date, no confirmation has been made as to the exact nature of the animal in question. If you witness anything unusual, contact animal control or call 911 immediately.

When I finished reading, I went to shower. Fetching gas wasn't that bad, but the fumes got into everything.

Afterward I put on my best shirt and pants and headed into the kitchen to get something to eat before going out. Abuela looked at me with sad, rheumy eyes. I knew she wanted me to stay in, or at least come home early. Tomorrow was Sunday, and she wanted me to go to the earliest Mass with them.

"Hector," she said. She bustled beside me, fetching a bowl for rice and caldo. I nodded and told her I'd be back before eleven.

"*Bueno,*" she said and ruffled my hair. I kissed them goodbye. Abuela clasped me on the shoulder and told me one more time to be careful of the chupi and not to get into trouble. I promised her and strolled out into the dark. Any minute the crew would roll up in Tony's car and we'd check out a movie or something.

When no one showed, I texted Tony, but my texts went unread. A few times I saw the text bubble open and it looked like he was typing, but then it would disappear. I texted the others, but got nothing. I walked the block over to Rogelio's.

Rogelio was outside, looking around. "Don't know," he said. "Maybe they ditched us for some honeys."

"Maybe," I said, but it didn't feel right. I kicked at a tuft of crabgrass in his front yard. "You still want to go out?"

He looked around. "Yeah."

We had started up toward Chester when we heard it. A long howl. Then another. We booked it back to my place, and my abuelo was at the doorway, waving us in. "*Corrale!*"

Abuela had the Tele-Noticias on. Something had happened in Tony's hood, but no one knew what. The news crews kept going over the same footage over and over again. Suddenly, one of the reporters, a petite brunette, announced that *Animal World* would no longer be doing a show in our area.

Abuelo, disgusted, shut the TV off. We'd have to wait for tomorrow's paper to know what happened, my abuela said.

I checked Facebook. Update after update of blurry pictures and an endless list of comments like "What happened?" and "Does anyone know what's up?" followed by lame-ass guesses. Twitter was the same, except for some pics and live feed of the news crews and police yelling at people to stay back. And I sure wasn't going to check Snapchat to find out what was under the bloody sheet.

The next morning, Rogelio was at our door, ready for church. Abuela nodded in approval. We walked to church, and Abuelo stopped by the bodega to get the paper. He handed it to me to read on the way.

LOCAL TEEN AND FAMILY MAULED, SERVICES TO BE HELD
At approximately 7 pm on Saturday, local teen Antonio (Tony) Luis Hernandez was mauled in his driveway. Neighbours said that they heard screams and then saw Antonio's father and mother run toward him.

"Something small but fast ripped them apart as soon as they stepped out. After that, I went inside and called the police," neighbour Josephina Gonzalez said.

Another neighbour, Hugo Jimenez, said that the carnage was so bad that he ran inside to save his children and wife from such a sight. As he crossed himself, Mr Jimenez said, "They were good people. And Tony was their only child. They are all gone now." As he spoke, several people nodded and demanded more police protection.

Josue (Chuy) Ortega voiced the concerns of his neighbourhood. "So, some guy lost his finger, and now we got a dead family. When is someone going to call it what it is? And how are we going to get rid of it?"

Services for the Hernandez family will be held tonight at the St. Anthony Cathedral. Father Pablo Pavón will receive donations in the family's name.

The stories continued.

SOURCES CONFIRM ANIMAL WORLD PULLED
Animal World is no longer scheduled to film in Kern County. Executives say it is out of respect for the Hernandez family. The Kern County mayor has reserved comment at this time.

We all stood silent for a long time. Tony was family. His mom and dad were like an aunt and uncle to me and Rogelio. I saw Abuelo wipe away a tear. I did the same. For once, Rogelio had nothing to say.

Finally, Abuela crossed herself and asked Abuelo if he still had the shotgun in the garage. The chupi had gone too far. Rogelio and I looked at each other. Rogelio ribbed me. "Abuelo and Abuela are OG!"

Abuela gave him a long, appraising look. She nodded. "Now let's go."

Shots Reported Near Site of Mauling

Gunshots were reported near the home of a family mauled to death by an unidentified animal. Police were called to investigate.

At this time, BPD confirm a shooting, but the perpetrator and target remain unknown. Officer Douglas said the area was scoured for shell casings and debris, but no evidence was found.

No New Sightings

Animal control and emergency services are hopeful that the unidentified creature, thought responsible for the death of a family and several pets, has left the area.

Though the creature remains uncaptured, authorities are optimistic that there will be no further encounters.

Lawsuit Could Cost Millions

The animal control officer mauled by an unidentified animal has retained council and filed suit against his supervisor and Kern county.

Rogelio and I eventually returned to gas duty. One night, when we set the pails down, Rogelio pulled out his phone. He read some Twitter posts, and I laughed. When I got home that night, Abuelo and Abuela had the paper waiting.

I had laughed too soon.

Animal Control Issues New Warning
Numerous reports of howling and property destruction have been confirmed, and several small animals have been found dead. The incidents appear linked to similar exsanguination attacks earlier this month, though there have been no sightings of the creature thought responsible.

Residents are urged to stay inside and to keep pets indoors after dark until further notice.

Abuela and Abuelo looked at each other. "I told you it was lonely," she said.

MASLOW MEETS THE MAYFLY MOON

Janet Smith

Janet Smith is an SFF/horror writer who lives on Vancouver Island with her husband. She is a graduate of the SFU Writer's Studio and is scheduled to complete the SFU Editing program in the fall of 2021. This story was born from all of the 2020 upheavals, including some serious health issues for both herself and her best friend's family that changed them forever. It's a reminder that as central as our human issues seem, there are other agendas at work that use, or disregard, humans altogether. Janet has had two short stories published in anthologies, and she was shortlisted in the BC/Yukon Short 2020 story contest. 'Maslow Meets the Mayfly Moon' was first runner-up for the 2020 Surrey International Writers' Conference Storyteller's Award. Janet can be contacted at janetksmith.com.

© 2021, Janet Smith

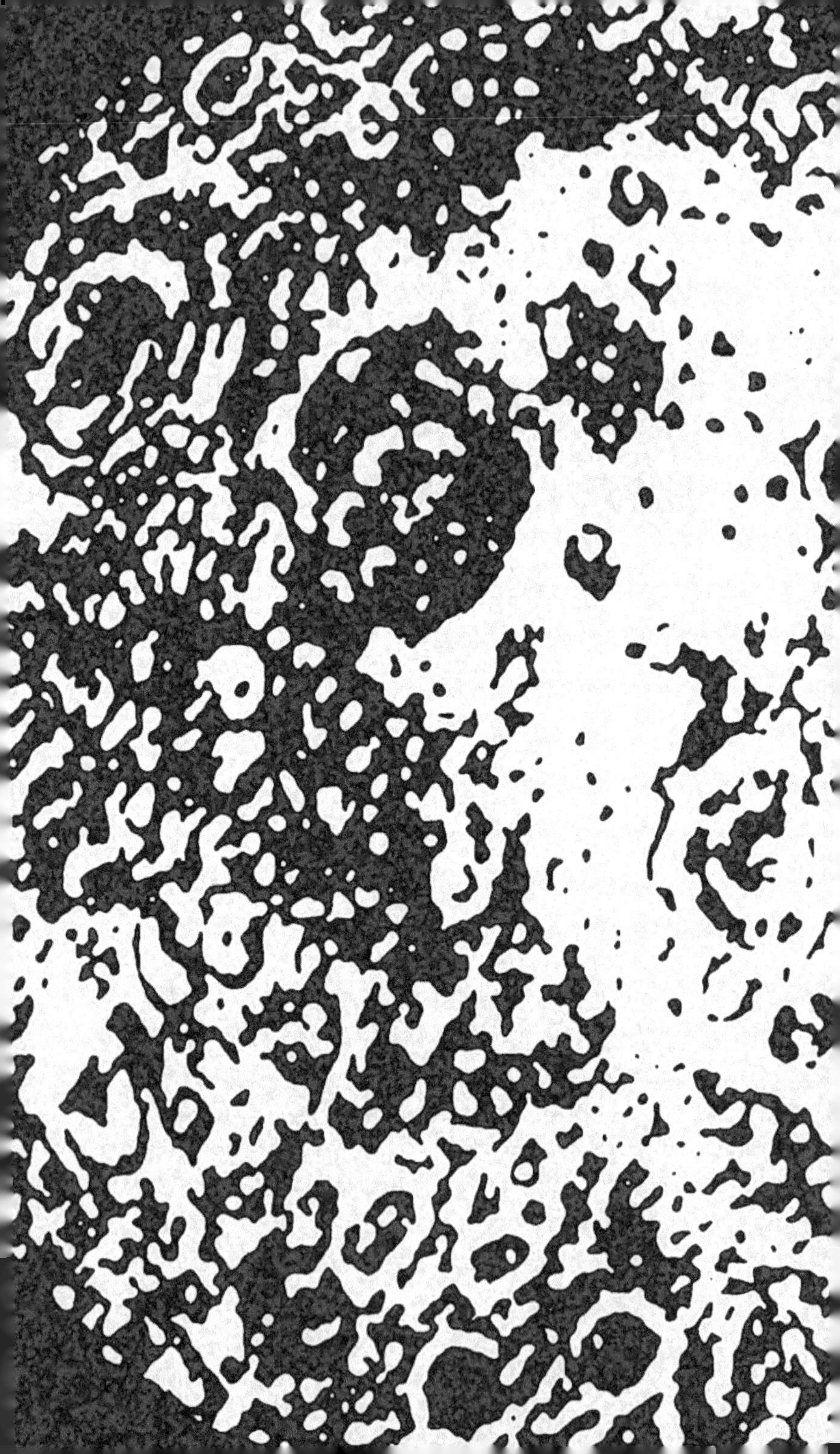

Maslow Meets the Mayfly Moon

Eril's canvas dominated the tiny living quarters. Not with its size, but in its vibrant contrast to the black surrounding it. The apartment walls, the ceiling, and the floor, along with every piece of furniture, had been 3D printed using the ebony sand of Stygia. As far as Sena Brevity was concerned, this perfect construction material made for a rather depressing decorative choice. She stepped toward the painting and peered at the kaleidoscope of colours in front of her. The brush strokes were short and precise. Beautiful. She stepped back, and the collage morphed into the face of a wistful woman. Brilliant.

Sena sighed at the talent on display, wistful herself as she measured her artistic shortfalls against her pride in this student's skill.

"I'm out of paint."

Sena spun around to find a dejected young man slumped on the couch behind her.

Eril held out a rolled-up tube of red pigment, not looking at her as he pulled his legs toward his chest and dropped his head into his knees. "Word got out."

She knew what that meant. The Marshall Council had categorized him as idle —— a status unacceptable in a colony less than sixty orbits old. Every sector within the city still juggled a crushing workload.

"Where?" was all she needed to say.

"Road crew. An eight-cycle stint starts tomorrow." The boy looked at her for the first time since entering his residence. His pallid face broke her heart.

She put her hands behind her back so he couldn't see her clenched fists. She knew who was responsible. "I'll fix this," she said as blood pounded in her ears. "The supply ship is coming. It'll be okay."

She made Eril a grilled cheese sandwich and left.

Stygia was a Cinderella moon in orbit around KOI-571.05, an exoplanet tracking a red dwarf sun through the Andromeda galaxy. In 2308, Sena, a naive art graduate, had joined the crew of a supply ship. She'd expected to find an established colony and citizens eager for culture, not an environment whose only colour came from the firm ebony sand that covered everything in every direction.

Statton Colony was nowhere to be seen from their landing site. The captain could only surmise it was a navigation failure. Rather than risk a search crew, he announced their supplies would be used to form a new Stygian colony named after his father, and the Marshall Colony became Sena's home.

The air was sweet, the water clean, and atop the few stone outcroppings, the crew discovered wild goat-like creatures they could domesticate for dairy and meat. This moon was a perfect fit for human settlement. Using its ever-present sand as raw material for their 3D printers, a city was erected, every aspect as black as space.

That was forty-five earth-years ago. Sixty orbits of Stygia's exoplanet around its red dwarf sun. Every orbit was a back-breaking, exhausting rotation where nourishment and protection of the body came before nourishment and enrichment of the soul. And after everything she'd done for this colony, they were going to take away her first really talented student, all over a quarter-cycle of lost labour.

"You can't go in there," said the man outside the supervisor's office. He half-rose from his chair; Sena blew past him.

The man inside closed his ledger and frowned at his ex-wife as she charged forward and planted her hands on his desk. "I wondered how long it'd take for you to show up. Before you start in on—"

"Start in? I'm not going to *start in* on you; I'm going to finish you, Rand. You were jealous of Eril when you and I were married, and now you're being spiteful, taking him away from me less than a month before our first show."

"Hey, turn it down a notch. I'm not the one who developed the rules for colony living. Everyone is expected to contribute. Even your precious Eril."

"He is contributing, Rand. Just because you don't appreciate his work … don't act like art is a waste of time."

Rand slammed his fist on the desk in front of her hands and stood to face her. "And you, don't act like art is a right. This colony may have reached a stage where it can afford to support an artist or two, but if they're not creating art, they need to work elsewhere. Why is that such a problem for you?"

"It's a problem because the supply ship should have been here by now. The paint is coming. It'll be here soon. You're punishing him, punishing me, for a delay completely out of our control. That's not the council's mandate; that's you being vindictive."

She stood her ground, but he'd worn her down during their marriage and she knew he could wear her down now. Their argument over the time and place for art within a society was as old as their relationship — a sore spot born of their first date. It had never healed. She played her last card. "You fought me over the blue painting. The one I made of us. If you agree to destroy it, I'll walk out of here, and Eril is yours for as many cycles as you want." There. She was all in.

After she'd held her breath longer than she thought possible, Rand finally said, "I can keep him off the list for a bit longer. But if he doesn't have paint in his hands by the time the Waterhouse project begins, he's no longer an art student."

Back at her art studio, Sena sat at her desk and whipped a pencil at the ceiling. It hit off-kilter and dropped straight to the floor. Five days. That's all she had. She flicked another one, using more wrist this time, driving the pencil point into the black tiles above her head. Nine black stalactites dangled precariously over her black desk — none of which gave her any idea how to get paint supplies to her studio in time to save Eril's future.

Even if the supply ship landed today, by the time everything was unloaded, the manifest was confirmed, and the items were distributed, it would be well past Rand's deadline. Once Eril was assigned to a work crew, he'd be committed to working there for a minimum of eight cycles. She had to admit her despair wasn't all about her student. The loss of his art was her loss too. Colour was as necessary to her as breathing. She hated this all-black moon.

Sena was about to throw another pencil when a voice carried across the studio.

"Are you there? Art Master Sena?"

It was her ex-husband's assistant, Faya. Sena squeezed her eyes shut. *No, no, Rand can't have changed his mind.* She clenched her jaw, ready to fight for the extra time she'd been given. "I'm in here."

The young man stepped forward and stopped a polite distance from her desk. "So sorry to bother you. I bought *The Forever Forest* when you were first given permission to paint. Please don't tell Rand. He wouldn't understand."

You might be surprised popped into her mind, but she verbalized her real fear. "Are you here to take Eril? He's not here. I have more time. Rand promised." She looked at the man in front of her. She was the same height and had a few pounds on him. She prepared to lash out if he moved to touch her.

Faya shook his head. "I want to help you. *The Forever Forest* is the first thing I see when I enter my unit. Against the blackness of this world, the lush greens of the forest produce a calm within me that's almost primal. I feel the cool air against my skin; I smell the chlorophyll from the leaves. In my mind, I dig the toe of my boot into the loam beside the path, and the moist dirt, worms, and grit fill my senses. For one split second, I am truly home."

With an ache in her throat, she opened her mouth to speak, but he waved away her attempt to respond.

"I have an idea that might help you." His eyes were shining. He was doing his best to stand still but couldn't contain his excitement. "You can pick up the paint directly from the supply ship."

If she met the ship when it arrived and helped unload, it could cut days off the wait time. She'd considered this idea before, of course, had even asked around to see if anyone could spare a hauler for the trip. No one would help. She shrugged. "Would if I could, young Faya."

Faya ran his fingers through his hair. "It's my job to assign the equipment to all the different sites. Right now there's a problem with the sewer access over on the west end of town, but half the equipment from the new bypass construction site has already been promised to the condo complex going up on the east side. Plus, the goats went crazy this afternoon, broke out of their pen, and headed for that rocky outcrop they seem to love so much. Rand has to pull people from his other projects, send them to fix the fence, then trudge them out into the plain to grab those bloody goats."

"Sounds complicated."

"That's the point," Faya said. "Equipment is getting moved all over the place. I have access to a loader the condo complex needs desperately. They'd easily take it in trade for a small hauler, and I could generate enough paperwork to ensure no one knows where either piece of equipment is supposed to be for at least four days."

"Rand won't find out?"

"I'm betting my job on it."

"When can we leave?"

He smiled and shook his head. "You, not we. I need to stay here and shuffle the paper. I'll be here at 3:00 am tomorrow." He hesitated. "Can you drive a hauler?"

"I can." She nodded. "How do you think Rand and I met?"

Faya arrived with the hauler at 3:10. It was bigger than Sena thought she needed, and it occurred to her that she could earn a few credits by delivering other items. She changed her mind when she remembered that Faya had taken a big risk to help her.

The night's cold bit into her face like a flesh-starved organism, and she scrambled up into the warmth of the driver's cabin.

After dropping Faya at his apartment, Sena slowly manoeuvred her way out of town. A dull glow from the red dwarf licked across the sand, creating an enchanted landscape before her as she moved north, away from the colony. The sun rose, and the sky erupted as if on fire. Sena became light-headed, and she slowed the hauler to a stop. Bold, demanding colours filled the sky, and she ached to capture every nuance of the glory. Here was her next project — this burst of light heralding a new day — one she could create for the upcoming exhibit.

Re-energized and eager to reach the landing pad, she pushed the hauler to move faster. But with few landmarks for reference, she felt like she was on a black treadmill, going nowhere fast. Early that afternoon, she was at the station house.

The supply ship hadn't arrived, giving her time to talk her way onto the crew. Sena turned off the hauler, and three men exited the station house and headed her way. She jumped down from the cabin, waved at the men, and walked toward them. Sena plastered a warm, seductive smile on her face, and when they smiled back, her confidence grew. She imagined driving away with a hauler full of paint — maybe within the next forty-eight hours, supply ship willing.

A man with binoculars turned to follow her tracks that led back toward Marshall. He yelled, but she didn't understand. He yelled again and his arm stabbed urgently toward the colony. The other men lifted their own set of binoculars and fixated on her home.

Sena did the same. She blinked. She blinked again. The colony was tilting. The left edge of the city had all but disappeared, and the buildings on the right lifted upward. Whatever was happening, it seemed to originate directly underneath the colony.

For one moment, time stopped. No sounds reached her. No dust rose into the air. Then she heard it. The clicking, whooshing sound of shifting sand. The sun's rays flashed and rolled with the heaving ground as the disturbance spread out from the city and rippled across the plain. Sena was mesmerized.

A siren pierced the air, breaking her stare and sending her heart to her throat. Sena took a quick glance toward the landing station. The sleepy base now crawled with men, yelling and running in all directions. Commands overlapped and were lost in the shifting sand-fire as it raced ever closer.

Sena ran for the transport. Even as she saw the front tires sink below the surface, she imagined driving to an outcropping of rocks and pushing goats aside as she made space for herself above the heaving sand. Her mind refused to acknowledge the disaster about to envelop her.

Every grain of sand vibrated and bounced against each other. Liquefaction pulled and sucked at everything on the surface. Beside the half-buried transport door, her leg sank into the surface of the moon. A high-pitched keening reached her ears — seconds passed before she realized she was the one screaming. With one leg fully immersed, her other leg was forced vertically, as if she were doing a high-kick to the side. Her left hip snapped against the tugging force of the vibrating sand.

Sena's head went under, and her airways filled with sand. As the fight left her body, a black calm filled her, revealing the grains of sand as tiny living creatures. They unfurled, clasped hands, and danced with the purest joy. Their celebration intensified into a sexual frenzy. The surface of Stygia became a swirling maelstrom of black, writhing, reproducing cells.

As the grains tired and pulled away from each other, a new bubble, teeming with fresh life, pushed its way to the surface of the moon. The new denizens burst upward, exploded onto the plain, and spread over the land. Their hunger flared, and the new life quivered and dropped back below the surface. Liquefaction of the colony provided ample sustenance for the denizens. With their offspring fed, it was the adults' turn to feast. Their long fast was over—there was flesh enough for all.

Quickly satiated, the last of the Stygians sighed and settled, leaving a flat landscape of black sand. Their dormant state would protect and sustain them until the next organic creatures colonized their moon. The collective would awake when the food source had grown ample enough to feed the native tribe once again.

Supply captain Kit Almos stepped onto the black expanse and signalled for the operator to lower the ship's hold. The Marshall Colony was supposed to be around here somewhere, but even with his most powerful binoculars, he could see nothing between him and the curvature of the moon's horizon. That meant two things: first, their bloody GPS was getting scrambled by the heavy metals in the moon's core; and second, wherever the colony was located, it was too far away for his team to spend precious energy and resources looking for it. He made the call. They'd build here. Their own colony. Maybe name it Marlon, after his father.

He bent down and ran the small black granules of the moon's surface through his fingers. "Get the printers out here. This sand is a perfect medium for building a city."

THE BUMBLEBEE FLASH FICTION CONTEST

© 2021, Alan Sincic

THE BUMBLEBEE FLASH FICTION CONTEST

Though short and sweet, flash fiction often delights the reader with a surprising sting that keeps us thinking about the story long after it ends. This year's contenders for the Bumblebee contest delivered carefully crafted prose that stung so good.

Final judge Bob Thurber deemed these winners a 'fun batch' that 'stood out from the beginning'. With many thanks to our judge, we are delighted to announce the winners of the 2021 Bumblebee Flash Fiction Contest.

First Place:
'Blind Maggie' by Alan Sincic

Runner-up:
'Solstice' by Melissa Nelson

Honourable Mentions:
'Pale Pony Express' by Lulu Keating
'The echo of light footsteps on parchment' by Kimberley Aslett

The 2021 shortlist in alphabetical order:

'Jump' by **Alex Reece Abbott**
'The echo of light footsteps on parchment' by **Kimberley Aslett**
'Les Mademoiselles' by **Lucia Gagliese**
'Green Panic' by **Lulu Keating**

'Pale Pony Express' by **Lulu Keating**
'The White Picket Fence' by **Val Melhop**
'No Time Like Now' by **Dan Micklethwaite**
'Solstice' by **Melissa Nelson**
'Blind Maggie' by **Alan Sincic**
'Geyser' by **Hannah van Didden**

A teacher at Valencia College, **Alan Sincic** *has fiction published in* New Ohio Review, *the* Greensboro Review, *the* Saturday Evening Post, Hunger Mountain, Prime Number, Big Fiction Magazine, Cobalt, Burningword, A-3 Press, *and elsewhere. His short stories have won contests sponsored by the* Texas Observer, Driftwood Press, Prism Review, Westchester Review, American Writer's Review, Vincent Brothers Review, *and the* Broad River Review.

After an MA in Lit at the University of Florida and a poetry fellowship at Columbia, he earned his MFA at Western New England University. Recently the opening chapter of his novel The Slapjack *won the 2021 First Pages Prize (Judge: Lan Samantha Chang, director of the Iowa Writer's Workshop). Come visit him at alansincic.com.*

$\mathcal{B}$LIND MAGGIE

BY ALAN SINCIC

The other hand—hammer hand—she folded into a fist. Held it. Trembled it there. *There,* she said. *Take that.* She made as if to thump the graven surface of the tray. The biscotti cowered. The fly buzzed, landed, buzzed again. She closed her eyes, tipped into the wind, listened for the fly to land. You don't mess, no, you don't mess with Maggie.

Blind Maggie is what they'd called her behind her back. She'd hidden it as long as she could. Inside the Slapjack—a cosmos she breathed into being every day at dawn—it was easy. Every implement belonged to her. Every manoeuvre she mastered. Even the regulars—in the silent morning, when they'd weary in to break the fast, smoke up the counter, rustle the newsprint into wobbly tablets that crackle in the hand—she knew who they were by the gait, and the rhythm of the breath, and the scent of the aftershave. The tick of the watch. The creak of the stool. The dust of the trade in the thread of the clothing—the rust or the gunite, the soot or the grain. So long as she presided over the diner and the yard—the henhouse and the woodshed and the garden—they were none the wiser.

Only when she ventured out did they notice the difference. At the Feed and Seed, how she pinched at the packet to suss out the name. At the grocer with the spices, how she'd sniff the lid, shake the jar as if to weigh the price. Maggie, who'd always been the fierce, who'd always dare the trucks to hit her when she speared off into the midday rush, they watched as she nudged up into the crowd at the crosswalk, felt her way up the shelf of sundries at the Five and Dime, fingered the tin dome of the talc and the bulb of the eau de cologne and the tube of lipstick, Ruby Red, Flame-Glo, cylindrical as the shell of a shotgun.

Maggie fought the sun to stay awake. Straightened herself. Parried the sound of the birds and the wind in the pine. Set herself to the task at hand, battled her way back to the time, to the place, to the day they found her in the rain, in a stand of oaks, a mile off the trail.

She'd followed the stream till the water rose and then—as the slurry ripped at her ankles and her knees—climbed up onto higher ground. Where? To hell with where. She was where she was. It was the world was in a tangle. Then by and by Cochrane come along. Out gigging bullfrogs round about dawn, and that dog of his. *Yip-yip*, she hears it, dog got a possum maybe, got a squirrel, but no. On the scent is what he is. Got himself a Maggie. *Yap-yap. Yap-yap-yap.* Up out the cane he comes, Cochrane. Slooshing up a swamp in the wake of them waders, dragging a sack of hoppers, high-stepping up the mucky bank. Up the trunk he runs a torch and *bingo*. There she is. Pressed up into the hollow of the oak, stick in hand, the mushrooms at her feet, the basket broken.

"Yo, Maggie. Been out shopping, I see."

"Digging you a grave, Cochrane. You and that dog of yours."

"You want I should fetch you an umbrella?"

"If I was made of marzipan. Look like I made of marzipan to you?"

Now Cochrane, he got the wit to run a dog, maybe, navigate a hand of poker, but a woman? "You … you got me. You got me there."

And that was that. And off he went.

Waiting for the clatter of the rain to cease, that's what she was about, waiting to where she could hear the road again, and the whistle at the depot, and the distant whine of the dredge at the base of the phosphate embankment to sound her back — through the woods, and over the fields, and under the shade of the oak in the yard — home.

So be it, right? You make do. You live the life you got. Stands to reason, really, when you think about it. Never would she admit, even to herself, the need for another set of eyes, no, any more than she would think to order up a sun to compensate for the one she lost.

Shhh. Listen. There it is now. You hear the buzz?

HOUSES

Matthew Nielsen

Matthew Nielsen, also known by the pen name Nuclear Jackal, is currently working on *Toni and Aberdeen*, a comic about time travellers living in an empty 2003 Vancouver. In this issue we bring you part one of 'Houses', a comic inspired by the many moves in Matthew's own life. He now lives in Canada, and as of this writing is in the process of moving house again. In the meantime, he uploads his illustrations to Instagram @nuclearjackal. Look for part two of 'Houses' in Issue 32, Autumn 2021, and while you wait, check out 'The Endless Drop' by Matthew and co-creator Minna Hakkola in Pulp Literature Issue 22, Spring 2019.

© 2021, Matthew Nielsen

BY MATTHEW NIELSEN
HOUSES
A COMIC ABOUT THE 11 OR SO PLACES I'VE LIVED IN

I HAVE LIVED IN ELEVEN HOUSES SO FAR.
I'VE ALSO BEEN TO TWO BOARDING SCHOOLS, BUT I DON'T COUNT THOSE EITHER.
THERE ARE ALSO HOUSES I STAYED AT FOR A FEW MONTHS DURING VACATIONS OR BETWEEN MOVES, BUT I DON'T COUNT THOSE.
PERHAPS I OUGHT TO SAY THAT I'VE LIVED IN ELEVEN HOMES IN MY LIFE.
MOVING HOUSE IS STRESSFUL ENOUGH, BUT DOUBLY SO WHEN YOU ARE DISTURBED BY CHANGES TO YOUR ROUTINE.
THINGS GET LOST, THINGS GET DAMAGED, AND THE CHANGES AREN'T ALWAYS FOR THE BETTER.
THERE ARE MANY ASPECTS OF MY LIFE I COULD TALK ABOUT, BUT THIS TIME I'D LIKE TO SHARE WITH YOU SOME MEMORIES I HAVE ASSOCIATED WITH EACH OF THESE HOUSES.
SOME MEMORIES I CAN'T QUITE ATTACH TO HOUSES. THESE WOULD BE GROUPED INTO OTHER CATEGORIES IN MY MIND.
I CAN'T REMEMBER WHICH HOUSE I LIVED IN DURING A VACATION TO DENMARK AS A CHILD, BUT IT MUST HAVE BEEN THE SECOND ONE.
HISTORY CLASS
DENMARK
HOLIDAYS
HOUSE
EDUCA

THE FIRST HOUSE I LIVED IN WAS IN DEVAUDEN (MONMOUTHSHIRE, WALES), A VILLAGE WITH A POPULATION OF ONLY A FEW HUNDRED.
MY PARENTS HAD BEEN LIVING THERE ONLY A FEW MONTHS WHEN I WAS BORN. THE THIRD CHILD IN THE FAMILY.
'BLUE BEAR'
'NOTHING'
I LIVED THERE FOR THE FIRST THREE YEARS OF MY LIFE, AND I SEEM TO HAVE A HANDFUL OF VAGUE MEMORIES.
I REMEMBER A DEAD PIGEON THAT HAD BEEN TAKEN OUT BY OUR CAT.
I REMEMBER RIDING MY TRICYCLE DOWN THE NEARBY LANE.
DAD
THERE WAS THAT TIME MY MUM WAS SCARED OF A MOUSE THAT HAD GOTTEN INTO THE KITCHEN.
I RECALL HER HOLDING A BROWN TUPPERWARE BOX AND STANDING ON A CHAIR LIKE IN THE CARTOONS.

WHAT I THOUGHT WAS MY EARLIEST EVER MEMORY TURNED OUT TO BE A DREAM.
IT WAS JUST ME SITTING ON MY MUM AND DAD'S KING SIZE BED.
MAKES SENSE, BECAUSE IT WAS IN A THIRD PERSON PERSPECTIVE.
I WONDER IF MY OTHER MEMORIES ARE REAL THEN?
MY PARENTS WERE GOOD FRIENDS WITH OUR NEIGHBOURS, AND REMAIN SO TO THIS DAY.
IT WAS THE ONLY TIME WE SOCIALISED THAT MUCH WITH OUR NEIGHBOURS. ALL THE OTHER TIMES WE KEPT TO OURSELVES, AND SO DID THEY.
MOVING DAY WAS ON MY THIRD BIRTHDAY. I DIDN'T KNOW WHAT WAS HAPPENING BUT I REMEMBER SEEING IT FOR THE FIRST TIME.
IT WAS AN OLD TERRACED VICTORIAN HOUSE WITH FOUR FLOORS AND A LARGE BACKYARD.
WE WERE NO LONGER IN THE VILLAGE, NOW IT WAS THE TOWN OF NEWPORT.
THE UNITED KINGDOM HAS SEVERAL 'NEWPORTS' AND SOUTH-WALES HAS TWO OF THEM. THIS WAS THE ONE IN GWENT.

AFTER A WHILE, OUR FAMILY ADOPTED A SHELTER DOG NAMED 'BLACKBERRY'.
UPON SEEING THIS NEW ADDITION TO THE FAMILY, OUR CAT WENT FROM BEING A HOUSE CAT TO AN OUTDOOR CAT.
SHE WOULD STAY WITH US NONETHELESS, EVEN THOUGH WE MOVED MANY TIMES DURING HER LIFE. SHE'D JUST LIVE OUTSIDE IS ALL.
AND IT TURNED OUT THAT TWO OF US ENDED UP BEING ALLERGIC TO CATS, SO THIS WAY WE COULD KEEP HER.
MY ELDEST SISTER GOT A PET SNAKE THAT SHE NAMED 'DIANA'.
SO ONE DAY WHEN I HEARD ON THE TELEVISION THAT 'DIANA HAD DIED', I RAN UP TO MY SISTER'S ROOM AND SAID:
TO WHICH SHE PROMPTLY REPLIED:
NO, NO, THEY MEAN PRINCESS DIANA.
HANNAH! YOUR SNAKE HAS DIED! THE TV SAID!
OH. THAT'S ALRIGHT THEN.

I DIDN'T HAVE A PROBLEM WITH THE FORMER PRINCESS OF WALES, I WAS JUST HAPPY THAT THE SNAKE WAS OKAY.
SHE ESCAPED ONCE, BUT CAME BACK A FEW MONTHS LATER ABOUT TWICE THE SIZE WE DIDN'T HAVE ANY SPIDERS AT ALL DURING THAT TIME.
MY PARENTS ALSO DECIDED TO RENOVATE THE OLD HOUSE IN ORDER TO HELP SELL IT.
ONE OF THE STEPS INVOLVED FIXING THE OLD FLOORBOARDS IN MY BEDROOM.
SO AS MY DAD WAS WORKING AWAY, I WENT OVER TO WALK AROUND AND SEE MY ROOM.
MATTHEW, STAY AWAY FROM THE CORNER!
THOSE FLOORBOARDS ARE LOOSE!
ABOUT 10 YEARS OLD
BEING BAD AT PAYING ATTENTION, KINDA DUMB, AND NOT SO GOOD AT HEARING IN THE FIRST PLACE, I WALKED OVER THERE.
AND PROMPTLY FELL THROUGH THE FLOORBOARDS.
IT WAS ABOUT AN 11FT (3.35M) DROP.
YES, IT HURT, BUT THANKFULLY I WAS BOTH LUCKY AND OBESE AT THE TIME, SO I GOT AWAY WITH ONLY HAVING A BRUISE ON ME BUM.
WHOMP!
EH'MHFLH...! WHAAA

A YEAR OR SO LATER, I STARTED GETTING REALLY INTO CREATING FANTASY WORLDS INSPIRED BY THE LIKES OF DRAGONBALL Z.
STEPHONIX
Card collection
Dork Wizzard
most common and weakest enemy. Nobody has seen a dork wizzard without disguize usaly
have 80 LP.
STEPHONIX
RARITY
I MADE A BUNCH OF 'COLLECTIBLE CARDS' AND GAVE THEM TO EACH OF MY CLASSMATES.
ORIGINALLY I CALLED IT 'FINAL FANTASY TRIVIA', EVEN THOUGH IT HAD ABSOLUTELY NOTHING TO DO WITH FINAL FANTASY.
ALSO I USED THE WORD 'TRIVIA' BECAUSE I DIDN'T KNOW WHAT IT MEANT, AND IT SOUNDED SO COOL.
A SWORD WARRIOR →
HE WEARS A GREEN JUMPER.
THE EARLIEST CARDS WERE EVENTUALLY DESTROYED BECAUSE I WAS WORRIED I'D GET ARRESTED FOR COPYRIGHT INFRINGEMENT.
I RENAMED IT 'STEPHONIX' AND WENT ON TO WRITE ABOUT 18 PLANETS FULL OF WAR AND ADVENTURE.
IT WAS AROUND THAT TIME WE MOVED A FEW HOUSES UP THE ROAD.
THIS WAS A HUGE CHANGE FOR THE FAMILY; WE SPENT YEARS IN THE OTHER HOUSE, BUT THIS ONE WAS, WELL...

KINDA SHITE.
WE WERE ONLY THERE FOR A YEAR OR SO, BUT THE BATHTUB EVENTUALLY PARTIALLY FELL THROUGH THE BATHROOM FLOOR.
GOOD THING NOBODY WAS IN THE ROOM IT FELL INTO AT THE TIME.
WORSE THAN THE HOUSE WERE THE EVENTS AROUND THIS TIME.
NEW PENNY
1
MY DAD'S JOB WASN'T GOING WELL, SO OUR FAMILY BUDGET BECAME QUITE CHALLENGING.
I FINALLY GOT DIAGNOSED WITH ASPERGER'S.
I ALSO STARTED SECONDARY SCHOOL, AND PROMPTLY GOT EXPELLED FOR PUSHING A TEACHER.
SO I WAS OUT OF SCHOOL FOR SEVERAL MONTHS.
THE CHILDREN'S BBC CHANNEL HAD 'CLASS TV' WHICH RAN EDUCATIONAL SHOWS, SO I ENDED UP LEARNING MORE FROM TV THAN SCHOOL ANYHOW.
Look and Read

JUST AS I STARTED GOING TO BOARDING SCHOOL FOR FOLK WITH ANTI-SOCIAL BEHAVIOUR ISSUES, IT WAS TIME TO MOVE AGAIN.
THIS TIME TO A VICARAGE.
WE KNEW THAT THE PREVIOUS OCCUPANT WHO LIVED THERE WAS A REVEREND, SO OCCASIONALLY WE HAD FOLK KNOCKING ON THE DOOR ASKING FOR CHURCH-RELATED THINGS.
SOME WERE PLEASANT, BUT A LOT OF THEM WERE BELL-ENDS.
WEARING A GOLD CHAIN
I'M A BIT BROKE AND WAS TOLD THE PRIEST COULD GIVE ME SOME MONEY?
JUST FOR SOME CIGGIES, IS ALL.
NOW WHAT THE REALTOR HADN'T TOLD US WAS THAT THE REVEREND WHO USED TO LIVE HERE WAS A PEDOPHILE.
I BELIEVE IT WAS SOME NEIGHBOURHOOD YOUTHS WHO BROUGHT IT TO OUR ATTENTION.
OI!
HEY, PEDO!
I'M NOT SURE IF WE GOT MORE VANDALISM THAN USUAL BECAUSE OF THIS, BUT WE CERTAINLY GOT PLENTY.

AND THEFT.
A LOT OF THEFT.
DURING OUR TIME IN THAT VICARAGE, WE HAD MULTIPLE THINGS STOLEN FROM OUR FRONT LAWN.
MY LITTLE BROTHER'S BICYCLE.
OUR JACK-O'-LANTERNS.
A LAUNDRY BASKET WE HAD USED TO COLLECT GRASS.
SOMEONE EVEN TRIED TO STEAL MY MUM'S CAR.
BUT ENDED UP SETTING IT ON FIRE INSTEAD.
LUCKILY IT WAS PARKED ACROSS THE ROAD FROM THE HOUSE.
IT MADE FOR A CURIOUS DISPLAY.

AFTER SOME TIME, E MOVED TO ANOTHER VICARAGE, THIS TIME IN CARDIFF.
VICARAGES WENT FOR LOW RENT, Y'SEE.
ON MOVING DAY THERE WAS AN ABSURD STREET FIGHT GOING ON OUTSIDE THE HOUSE.
FIRST IT WAS TWO YOUNG WOMEN.
THEN THEIR BOYFRIENDS STARTED FIGHTING EACH OTHER.
THEN THEIR BOYFRIENDS' MOTHERS STARTED FIGHTING. SOON THERE WERE TWENTY PEOPLE INVOLVED!
THE OLD BILL BLASTED THEIR SIRENS FROM FAR OFF AND THE LOT SCAMPERED.
GOOD WORK, CONSTABLE.
NEE-NAW!

OUR CAT WOULD LIVE IN A LITTLE WOODEN CATHOUSE THAT MY DAD BUILT FOR HER.
ON COLD NIGHTS, HE'D EVEN PUT A HOT WATER BOTTLE IN THERE FOR HER.
WHEN SHE DIED AT AN OLD AGE, WE BURIED HER IN THE FRONT GARDEN OF THIS HOUSE.
THUD.
THAT DAMN PAINTING FELL AGAIN.
HMM.
ONE EVENING WE HEARD A NOISE WHILST WATCHING A MOVIE.
A WHILE LATER, A POLICEMAN KNOCKED ON THE DOOR.
IT TURNS OUT THE NOISE WAS A WOMAN WHO HAD DRUNKENLY CRASHED INTO OUR FENCE.
I THINK SHE LIVED; NEVER FOUND OUT.

OUR HOUSE WAS NEAR THE SHOPS, SO OUR GARDEN FILLED UP WITH GARBAGE.
THE VANDALISM CONTINUED, AND THE POLICE DID NOTHING TO HELP.
HOWEVER, THEY DID MAKE SURE TO TELL MY DAD THAT THEY'D LOCK HIM UP IF HE RESORTED TO VIGILANTISM.
I WAS COMING HOME FROM BOARDING COLLEGE EVERY OTHER WEEKEND AND WOULD OFTEN FIND NEW SIGNS OF DAMAGE TO THE VICARAGE.
AND THE MOULD IN MY BEDROOM, OBSCURED BY MY BOOKCASES, GREW AND GREW.
WE EVENTUALLY REMOVED IT, BUT IT TOOK AGES TO SHIFT EVERYTHING.
MY DAD GOT A BETTER JOB AND WE WERE FINALLY ABLE TO MOVE OUT.
WE WENT BACK TO NEWPORT, THE OUTSKIRTS THIS TIME. A MUCH BETTER PLACE.
BEDROOM
OFF AGAIN

MY EDUCATION WAS DIVIDED UP INTO:

PRIMARY SCHOOL (AGES 4 TO 12)
SECONDARY SCHOOL (12 TO 16)
SIXTH FORM/COLLEGE (16 TO 19)
UNIVERSITY (19 TO 21)
WHEN I MOVED INTO THIS HOUSE, I WAS IN MY LAST YEAR OF COLLEGE.
OUR NEIGHBOURS WERE PLEASANT. THE FIRST ONES WE HAD SINCE THOSE GRUMPY GITS THREE HOUSES AGO.
THOUGH THEY DID HAVE COOL FROGS
THE NEIGHBOUR TO OUR LEFT WORKED AS A POLICE OFFICER, AND ALWAYS GREETED US WITH SMILES.
AND THE NEIGHBOUR TO OUR RIGHT ACTUALLY HAD A CHICKEN COOP IN HIS BACK GARDEN. HE EVEN GAVE US EGGS ONCE.
DURING THE SUMMER AFTER MY GRADUATION FROM COLLEGE, I DISCOVERED SOMETHING STRANGE AND WAS PROMPTLY DIAGNOSED WITH TESTICULAR CANCER.
LUCKILY I FOUND IT JUST IN TIME. NO NEED FOR CHEMO, JUST A BIT OF SURGERY, AND IT WAS ALL SORTED.
HERE AND GONE IN ONE WEEK.

HOWEVER, A FEW DAYS AFTER THE SURGERY,
ON MY BIRTHDAY TOO, MIGHT I ADD,
HAD TO ATTEND THE INDUCTION TO UNIVERSITY.
NOW THAT WAS A SORE DAY.
FILL OUT THIS, THEN PROCEED TO ROOM 206.
HEMF.
OUR HOUSE WAS NEAR A LOUD AND BUSY ROAD, BUT IT WAS A GREAT BARGAIN SEEING AS IT WAS A HOME FREE OF VANDALISM.
TESCO
AS TIME PASSED, THE FAMILY'S MONEY SITUATION GOT COMPLICATED AGAIN.
SO, SEEING AS MY TWO OLDER SISTERS HAD ALREADY MOVED TO CANADA, IT WAS DECIDED THAT MY MUM AND YOUNGER BROTHER SHOULD TOO.
MY DAD AND I PLANNED TO MOVE OVER AFTER I HAD FINISHED UNIVERSITY.

§

'Houses' will continue in Pulp Literature *Issue 32, Autumn 2021.*

ALLAIGNA'S SONG: OBURAKOR

JM Landels

JM Landels *is torn between travelling the world to teach writing and swordfighting, and never leaving her idyllic farm in Langley, BC. Her debut series, fantasy bestseller* Allaigna's Song: Overture, *and the sequel,* Aria, *are available from Pulp Literature Press and Amazon. You can follow her adventures with pen and sword at jmlandels.stiffbunnies.com. In this issue we present the final part of the novella* Allaigna's Song: Oburakor, *which is set between the second and third novels of the trilogy. If you missed the first two parts, catch them in* Pulp Literature *issues 27 and 29.*

© 2021, JM Landels

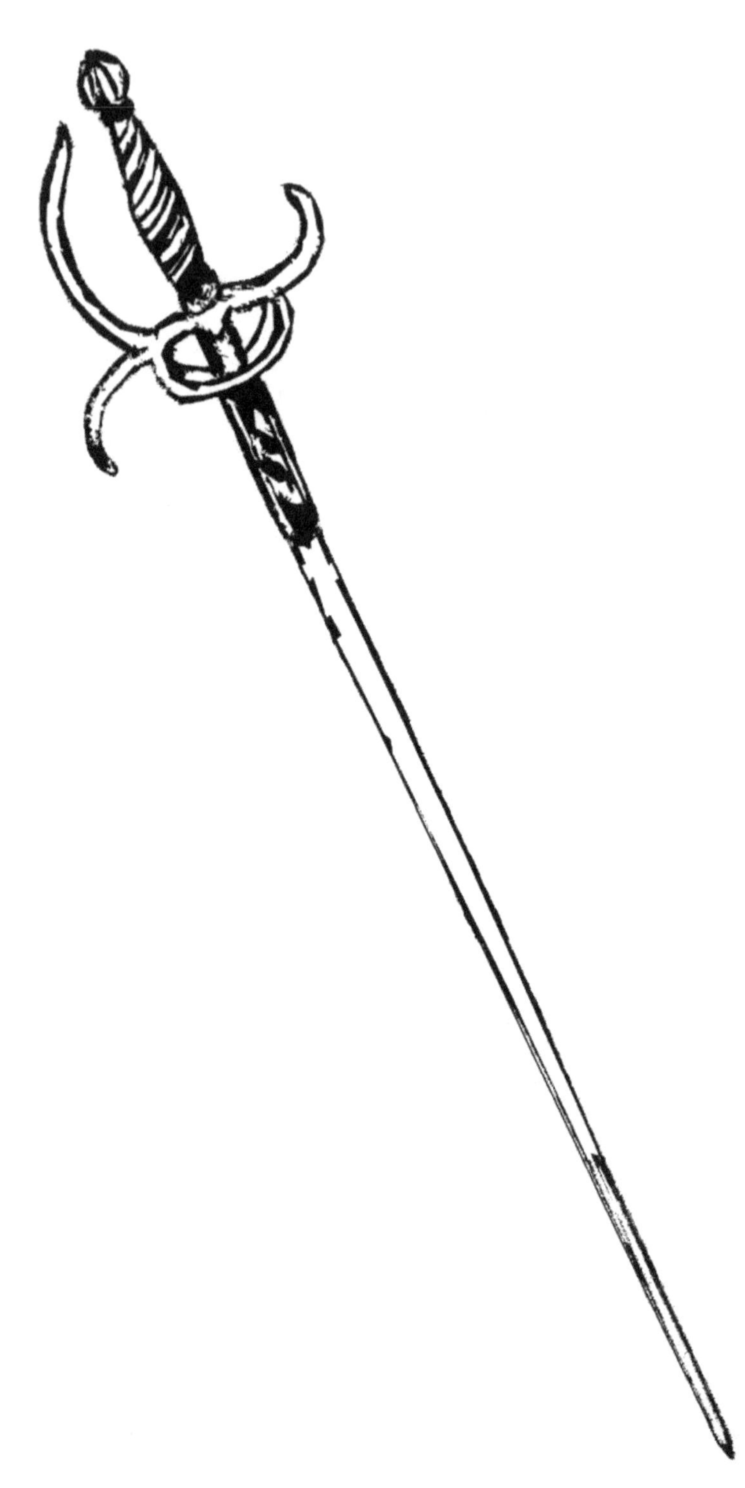

Previously in *Allaigna's Song: Oburakor* . . .

Following six years in the Brandishear Rangers, Allaigna has mustered out. Upon leaving, she receives a mysterious note from her grandfather offering her a private commission. The task takes her and a handful of mercenaries to an unknown wasteland with an incomplete map and a task to explore the ancient arcane Lothgates, long thought to be inactive. After witnessing the cataclysmic destruction of a gate, Allaigna and her companions are forced to travel overland to the nearest mountain pass to make it home.

Verse 6

Olenbry

We marched, five leagues a day or more, while the clearmoon went from dark to bright, and half-dark again. The map allowed us to avoid the larger settlements — what few there were — and we filled in the details of scattered crofts we came near in the spare and hilly landscape. And gradually, as the days wore on, the air got thinner and colder, and our steps carried us higher up the foothills to the feet of the Ursumma mountains.

I sat with my back to the largest boulder I could find, meagre shelter though it was from the wind that came skidding down off the mountain behind me. The small gully we chose to shelter us for the night did nothing to stop the wind, which had switched direction from south to west. Imerian and Goff went in search of brush for firewood, and the rest of our small party took what protection we could from the landscape as we sorted our belongings, consumed scant rations, mended clothing, and attended to our weapons.

Rennielle sat opposite me, running a lump of beeswax over her bow. Since her revelations, attitudes towards her had changed. Goff was outwardly hostile, almost hurt. The rest were friendlier, as if knowing that she was actively trying to foil the mission made her less of a personal threat. For myself, I wasn't sure. There were things I still didn't understand. The question was how to draw out answers. Perhaps bluntness was the key.

"So," I said to her, "how *did* you manage to fool Goff all this time?"

She looked up at me from under eyebrows so pale they almost were not there. "Please," she said. "Do not tell me you've never seduced a man for purposes other than amusement."

I shrugged. "Never for so long." In truth, I didn't need to. What a charm sung over a mug of beer couldn't achieve, a suggestive tune hummed in the ear usually could. But such a lengthy scheme—to become Goff's lover and then his prisoner, just to ensure he'd take her along ...

I mused out loud. "He'd never take his lover on a suicide mission. So you did something—not heinous enough that he'd kill you. But clearly he couldn't just arrest you and leave you behind. Why?"

She looked up again and smirked.

I continued. "What did he say in his pillow talk that high command in Rheran must never know?"

She slid her longbow back into its oilskin sleeve. "Why under the great sky would I tell you that?"

"Because," I said, "it's a dangerous journey, and you want someone other than yourself to know."

"No," she said. "I don't. If that knowledge goes with me to the grave, all the better for both of us."

"You're not worried Goff may think that too?"

"If he hasn't killed me by now, he won't."

She stood, wrapping her cloak around her against the wind, and strode up out of the gully. At that moment, Goff and Imerian returned with an armload each of prickly scrub branches. "My watch," said Rennielle over her shoulder.

I put away the stone I'd been using to de-burr my sword and took out my flint to start a fire. Harthor and Imerian could easily start one magically — and so could I if I chose to reveal my ability — but we had been conserving magical energies. Even the effort of producing a flame might cost them needed arcana if we had to defend ourselves.

"We need a shelter," announced Imerian, sniffing the air like a hound. "There will be snow."

None of us were dressed for it. It had been a warm Patalis in sunny Brandishear, but now we were in the eastern foothills of the Oburakor range.

"We'll need to stretch out two cloaks, make a windbreak, and share the rest between us," said Goff.

That irritated me. "Why at least did you not come prepared for the weather?" I snapped.

He grabbed me by the elbow, hauling me away from the others. "You've had a hornet up your arse for the last two weeks, cousin. If you've got something to say to me, spit it out."

I wrenched my elbow out of Goff's grip and strode another several paces uphill. Rocks and scree tumbled behind me, a flurry to match the flakes of snow that were now twisting out of the sky. Here the wind whipped loose strands of hair into my face, but at least it blew my words away from the others, sheltered as they were in the deeper part of the gorge.

"Why are we here, Goff?"

His eyes disappeared in the evening gloom — all I could see of his face was the swathe of black under his brow, darker than the rest. "I've told you everything about the mission, Allaigna."

"Not what we are doing here," I said. "Why us? Why are *we* here? You. Me. The Prince's kin. And of all of them. Why us?"

He shook his head, which registered as a slight blur of the dots of snow stuck in his hair. "Why you? I can only assume you confronted him with your claim to the throne," he said.

I sucked in an ice-coated breath. "You didn't … you asked him to legitimize you?" I was dumbfounded.

"Not in so many words."

I made an expectant gesture that I wasn't sure he could see in the gloom.

He continued. "I presented a patent of arms. Containing —"

I finished for him. "Let me guess. A falcon, and a horse. No, worse than that. A falcon and a white horse."

The red horse was Chanist's blazon, but the white was his elder brother's, the late Prince Girondrey's. Paired with the falcon of Brandishear, it would have been Girondrey's crest once he assumed the throne — if he hadn't been assassinated.

"I'm not such a fool as that," he hissed into the wind. "It was the white horse and thistle."

"Ah." It was a less obvious but no less foolish claim. The

cardoon denoted descent from the female side. That still made it a claim to the throne. "And that is somehow better?" I asked. "Reminding him of the niece he has locked away with the Errelites? Whose claim is stronger than his own?"

"I don't want the damned throne, and neither does she. I just want my mother acknowledged."

Perhaps, but with the madness, the paranoia, my grandmother had spoken of, Chanist wouldn't see it that way. I told him so.

He grimaced. "Yes, I gathered that much from this suicidal mission. And what did *you* do to earn his wrath?"

I looked a quarter turn away, the wind clearing the hair from my face but pelting it instead with stinging snow. "I was hoping you could tell me." I sat on my haunches, mostly to diminish the wind but also to take my eyes away from his face. "Existing was enough, I think."

Instead of squatting beside me, he hauled me up by my elbow. I jerked it away from him.

"You were leaving his service," Goff said. "Why not let you go home? I think he was trying to assuage his conscience."

"How so?"

"By sending you after me."

I began to laugh. Goff's ego hadn't diminished in all these years. To think I'd been sent as his protector … It was absurd. Or at least I hoped it was. I reached down to the dry and prickly plants that somehow clung to this dry, cold land, and pulled up a bundle. Brittle and light, insubstantial as bird bones, the stalks would crumble to powder at the slightest pressure. But the seed pods, armed with spikes a hedgepig would envy, were dense and heavy.

"Come," I said, gathering more despite the prickles. "These will burn well."

We turned back down the hill with armloads of prickle bushes.

"More fuel," I said to the others crouched around the fire.

I tossed a small bush in. It crackled with a satisfying roar, but was gone in seconds. I was about to throw in another when Imerian stopped me.

"Wait." He used his knife to flick out a seed pod from the fire, charred but intact. He crushed it on a flat rock with the side of his knife and a rich smell, like roasting chestnuts, drifted into the air. He stuck the tip of the knife into the crushed meat and put it to his tongue. "Edible," he concluded, "and delicious. Are there more?"

"How do you know it's not poisonous?" asked Goff.

"Nothing as well-armoured as that needs to be poisonous. And anything that good needs armour. The harder the nut, the better the meat."

We gathered more of the strange thistles till full dark, then spent just as long picking out the bristly seed pods.

Imerian roasted them on his griddle, and I watched the seeds dance and crack over the flames. When we ate them at last, they were indeed delicious. And more filling than they appeared. How odd to be saved from hunger in this barren land by the lowly thistle. I glanced at Goff, but he was staring at Rennielle, an impenetrable expression on his face.

The days of marching—our only respite the moments when we stopped to eat, piss, or briefly sleep—were made even longer by the unexpected gullies and ridges that led us off course and the small rivers, not marked upon the map, which needed fording. It was cold, and it grew colder the higher we mounted the foothills. Our clothing, made for sunny Rheran autumn, proved less and less sufficient.

Rennielle shot a mountain deer, no bigger than a young goat, and Imerian skinned and butchered it. It was only food enough for three days for the six of us, and tough and unappetizing at that, but it provided a reeking, untanned hide for Olenbry, who was suffering most from the cold.

The day after that she was cold no more, but feverish. It took all of Imerian's skill with his diminishing pouch of herbs and medicines to keep her on her feet. We argued hotly over whether to rest a day and allow her time to convalesce, but it was Olenbry herself who stood up and, in a voice as thick as the snow that covered the ground, announced she would rather die on her feet than spend one day more than necessary with a pack of arseholes like us in a forgotten dunghole like this.

Two days later, Goff too was shivering with fever, Rennielle's seldom-used voice got quieter still, and my own throat burned. Olenbry could barely walk.

And on the afternoon of the twentieth day since we'd arrived in this land, with the light fading fast, footsore, exhausted, and half of us ill, the ragged stone towers of Ravensholt Pass rose into view.

Another debate broke out: whether to push on to the pass and find shelter there in the deserted keep, or wait till full day the next morning, when the climb up the snow-covered road would be easier.

Rennielle, standing apart as always, saw what we did not. "It isn't deserted," she said, the effort of speaking leaving her tone even flatter than normal.

Harthor cast his gaze up the slope and nodded. "There is smoke coming from the right-hand gate tower. Someone is there."

"Good," said Olenbry. "A fire between four walls is exactly what I need." She wrapped the deerskin tighter around her shoulders and directed her slow, pained walk upwards.

"No," said Goff. "We camp here tonight."

Olenbry didn't turn to glare at him, but the stiff set of her back said enough.

He walked to face her, and us all. "Aerach and Holc do not man these passes anymore." He looked at me, and I nodded confirmation. "So that fire is from . . . what? Essaruk villagers out for a stroll in the mountains? There are no farms or towns or even inns here. That tower either contains travellers like us" — with a glance, we acknowledged the unlikeliness of that — "or it is garrisoned. Tonight we rest, tomorrow we scout. And then we decide how to approach."

Olenbry's shoulders sagged, but she made no move forward or back. The rest of us began setting yet another makeshift camp for the night, this one leeward of the densest clump of trees we could find.

As we had for the last few nights, we settled Olenbry in the middle, Goff and Rennielle to one side of her, and Imerian and Harthor to the other while I took first watch. When the moon was a handspan past the horizon, I nudged Harthor awake and slipped into the warm spot beside Imerian. Harthor would do the same to Rennielle later on, she to Goff, and he to Imerian.

Dawn came bright, the sun dazzling off the snow. The second thing I noticed was that Imerian still slept beside me, unreplaced by Goff. I nudged him awake with aching bones, reluctant to leave what little warmth there was next to him. The crunch of footsteps behind me killed that lethargy in an instant, and the rush of cold air as I stood woke the others.

It was Rennielle, and not alone. In front of her she frog-marched an Essaruk woman who was bleeding freely from a gash on her temple.

Rennielle pushed the woman to the ground. She sprawled face first in the snow, then struggled to come to her knees. Her hands were bound behind her back, so she could only shake her head to clear the snow from her face.

"Found her sneaking up on us." Rennielle picked up a handful of snow, washing her hands with it. It fell to earth in pink spatters.

"Why didn't you wake us?" Goff croaked.

Rennielle gave him a look. "It was under control," she said coolly, though the damp patches and scuffs of mud on her knees and cloak told me the hunt was not effortless.

"Now we know who is in that tower."

There was a moan from behind us. It was Imerian, bent over Olenbry. "She's gone," he said.

Verse 7

Dortallah

We closed Olenbry's cold eyelids and pried rocks from out of frozen ground to build a cairn for her while Rennielle guarded her captive. There was no fuel to make a pyre, and no time to hold a wake. With a burning throat I sang a funeral song, shorter than she deserved, and left it ringing in the air when we at last turned our attention back to Rennielle's prisoner.

Though my throat was raw, my voice almost gone, I had a hunch. "Let me talk to her," I said to the others as we packed up our camp.

"Talk all you want. You do not speak Sarrukken—she will not hear," retorted Rennielle.

"I have a gift with languages. I picked up some from the priest who died." It was only partially true. The Leisanmira gift of tongues is not so much a talent of speaking but of listening. The cadence and melody of a language is like a song, and music is something I could turn to my own ends. "Ask her to speak," I said.

"And say what?"

"Anything."

Sarrukken, a round and musical language, sounded hard and guttural in Rennielle's mouth. She said something, and the woman responded. I made a rolling motion with my hand, asking her to keep going while I hummed, following the pitch and tone, the stops and trills, the rhythm and metre, with my voice. When I found a pattern I repeated it, moulding it into the verse and chorus of a charm that I inhaled into my vocal chords. After three iterations, I opened my mouth to speak in Ilmarin.

What came out was Sarrukken. "My name is Allaigna," I sang. "What is yours?"

The woman's eyes opened wide, whether in surprise or fear I couldn't tell.

"Dortallah," she said, though my ears heard 'Wind Walker' through the music's charm.

"Dortallah," I said, and once I said it, it became a name and not a meaning in my ears. "Dortallah, I apologize for my companions' treatment of you. We are tired, ill, and far from home, and cannot risk meeting strangers who may be hostile. What were you doing around our camp?"

The woman lifted an eyebrow. "What are you doing in my country?"

I pushed away grief and gave her a hint of a smile. "Please. As we are at the advantage here, we will ask questions first, and give you answers later." *If we like yours*, I didn't need to add. My smile disappeared. "We have lost a friend today, and are not in a forgiving mood."

She touched a hand to her chest and then her forehead, in what seemed a ritual gesture. "I am sorry for your loss. May your friend find peace in the Mother's arms."

Rennielle frowned and seemed about to say something. I lifted a restraining hand. "Thank you," was all I said, and waited.

"In truth," she said, looking at the ground she knelt on, "all I wanted was to steal some bread."

"We have none," I said.

She looked up, her green eyes wide once more, and wet. "Please," she said. "Let me go. My children will be awake and hungry."

"Children?" Where in these forbidding foothills would a family live? "How far away are your children?"

Her lips closed. She would not give that secret away.

I settled on my haunches to look her in the eye. "We are not here to do you or your offspring harm. We just want to go home, and the closest way is that mountain pass. Do you know the way through?"

She looked wary again, which I took for a yes.

"Get us safely through there," I said, "and you can have all the meat we have left."

I could see Rennielle about to object again. But we had one less mouth to feed and could live one day without food if it got us into the Ilmar.

Dortallah nodded. "I will show you," she said.

The charm I'd sung was wearing off, and it became harder and harder for Dortallah and I to understand one another. Nevertheless, I gleaned a few bits of information as we followed her through the snow. The armies of Oburakor were moving, it seemed, fortifying mountain passes, preparing to defend its borders. And as they swept from the northern and central plains and cities to the mountains, they had, as all hungry armies do, cleaned out the larders of their people along the way. Dortallah's family holding, a small, self-sufficient commune nestled at the foot of the pass, had been picked clean.

"How do we know this woman's not leading us into a trap?" asked Goff. "Are we not the invaders her people are defending against?"

"If she does," said Rennielle, "we will at least kill her before we are killed, and her children will truly starve." She repeated this in Sarrukken, just to be sure Dortallah heard.

The woman smiled. "Why would I give you and your food to the army?"

"Are you not afraid we are spies?"

She spun to glare at me. "Spy? Yes, spy for your people. Tell them why invade country with no food, no wealth, bad weather. Essaruk king or foreign king—we starve the same."

The translation charm was almost done. I took her large calloused hands in mine, hoping the contact would keep understanding alive. "We do not want to invade," I said, speaking slowly. I glanced at the others, wondering if I could or should speak for them. No matter, I was. "We will do everything in our power to prevent this. I swear."

She looked moved for a second, then shrugged. She took her hand from mine and touched my forehead. "You hot."

"Yes," I said. "We've been sick. All of us."

"Stick out tongue," she said and, without asking, poked me under the jaw with her cold finger. "Is cradle cough. Babies get. Not people."

"Like red fever," Imerian murmured. "A once-in-a-lifetime disease. Adults don't get it because we survived it as children. But we never had this 'cradle cough'. And I don't know what medicines or charms will cure it."

"How do you treat it?" I asked Dortallah, putting music back into my tired throat to extend our comprehension of one another.

"Visit a priest. She bless."

"We have no priest. Is there anything else?"

She listed words that had no translation, along with 'tea'. We looked at her dumbly, and at last she pointed to a scraggly juniper bush. Imerian grabbed a branch and pointed at the bark, greenery, and berries in turn. She pulled off a berry and handed it to him, then held up all ten fingers.

"Tea, made of ten berries. What else?" I asked

Two more incomprehensible words. She shrugged, looking around. "Not grow in winter."

"What about willow bark?" I asked.

She shook her head violently. "No! Make worse."

I glanced at Imerian. I didn't know how much he understood of our exchange, but the stricken look in his eye gave a hint. He had given Olenbry a tiny portion of his precious supply of willow bark last night to ease the pain in her limbs.

We had juniper at least. That on its own might help.

"We need to go home," I said.

She nodded, and led us further down the ravine. We followed. Where the path turned left behind another clump of juniper, she stopped and pointed. "Follow. Door into keep at end. Army not know."

Imerian passed her the frozen bundle of venison. I reached into my scrip, where I still carried ten gold falcons—my severance pay.

I pressed two into her hand. "Thank you," I said in Sarrukken. It wasn't coin of her realm, but gold was gold, and her eyes widened.

"Wait," she said as Harthor and Goff started up the path. From her pocket she took out a small leather wallet. Unfolded, it held needles, thread, and small iron tools. From a pocket she withdrew a single pressed leaf shaped like a spear head. *"Wishtah"* she said, and I recognized it as one of the other ingredients she'd tried to tell us about. I could tell it was valuable by the way she held it.

"With juniper," she said. "It help more."

"Thank you," I said again, and took both her hands in mine.

VERSE 8

THE KEEP AT THE PASS

The door was a low wooden one set behind a natural spur in the rock face. Harthor pulled the rope handle, but the door didn't budge. He put his shoulder against it instead, and it gave with a scraping complaint. It was odd to have an outer door that opened inward—much harder to defend—and I concluded the builders and current lords of the keep knew nothing of its existence.

The rough-hewn tunnel behind the door was dark. "Harthor, Rennielle, you have the best eyes. What can you see?"

"Very little," said the former. "But I'll go first."

I considered humming a charm to cast light, but if Harthor was not going to expend his magical energy, I was hesitant to reveal my own.

The passage was low, with roots and rocks that reached down to knock our heads if we straightened. We progressed single file, each with a hand on the wall and one on the ceiling. Only Olenbry would not have had to crouch through here. My eyes blurred and my throat tightened. *Mourn later,* I instructed my heart.

We descended, then climbed, then climbed again narrow steps cut out of stone. And then we stopped. The stairs ended on a level area where we could all stand straight and still not touch the ceiling, but the walls were solid rock around us.

In the darkness someone rustled in a pack, and the sound of flint striking was followed by a blue spark and a tiny ember as Imerian lit a match string.

"You've had that all along?" Goff asked, his voice even harsher with incredulity and shortness of breath.

Imerian shrugged as he held the burning wick above his head. "I've been keeping them dry for emergencies."

The faint glow gave only enough light to see the walls around us — which seemed even closer — and the vast darkness above our heads. It was a chimney, or a dry well shaft, with no upper opening in sight. But just at the edge of the match's light, the end of a rope hung, swaying in the faint breeze created by our movement below. It was a thick one, with a large knot at the end.

"Lift me up," said Rennielle.

Goff wrapped his arms around her upper thighs and heaved, staggering more than he ought to under her tall but slight mass.

"Higher," she said.

I squeezed around to Goff's front and grasped one of Rennielle's legs by the knee and calf. He switched his grip to match mine, and in the tight chimney we lifted her till her knees were at our shoulders. I could smell Goff's breath on my face, and it reeked of hunger and illness. His muscles trembled, and I could feel the heat of his fever, still not abated.

"Got it." Rennielle's weight lessened as she grasped the rope and tugged. "Let go."

A moment later she'd pulled herself out of our grasp, her boots barely missing my face as they swung out to meet the wall of the chimney.

"What do you see?" croaked Goff.

"Nothing." At that point, Imerian's match went out. "Less than nothing."

There were noises that I took to be Rennielle climbing higher while Goff and I stood, preparing to be human bolsters should she fall.

Her voice came back again, farther away, but echoing through the stone chamber. "There's a lid."

More scuffling noises echoed down, followed by grunts and an Ilvanin curse. A square of dim blue light opened above, partly obscured by the form of Rennielle climbing through. She disappeared, then stuck her head back through the opening.

"It's a cellar, but it's dusty. There's an old evenlamp that barely works. I'm going to have to close the trap door or the rope won't reach." With that her head disappeared and the chimney went black again.

There was some arguing about who would go up the rope next and, more importantly, who would go last. For Rennielle was as tall as I and had still needed a boost from Goff and me to reach the rope dangling from the trapdoor above. Imerian had a short length of braided leather we tied to the larger rope, but even still, it was only long enough that I could just grasp it, standing on my tiptoes. And would it hold one of us?

"I'll go last," said Goff. "I'm tallest." In the blackness of the tunnel I couldn't see his expression, but I could hear it in his voice: the resignation of a commander, the determination to save his troops. Except we weren't his to command.

"You will not," I said. "You're feverish still, and weak. You are also, with your cuirass and greaves, the heaviest amongst us. I doubt that cord will hold you. You will go up next, and Harthor behind you." I turned in the dark to where I felt the mage stood. "Do you have some charm or cantrip you can affect to lessen his fall should he slip?"

"Easily done, but I can only cast it upon one of us."

"We are all in better strength than Goff," came Imerian's voice. I felt him turn to me. "You and I are of a height, Allaigna. Will you allow me to go last?"

I shook my head, then remembered he couldn't see me. "No. I'm lighter than you, and I was a champion vaulter as a youth." This was a lie. Now that I was near six feet tall, I could vault upon a courser's back, but as a short child I struggled getting on my stubby pony. But he didn't need to know that.

As Imerian boosted Goff up the rope, I began to hum the tune I had formulated so many years ago to make the training swords feel lighter in my arms and to let me leap far longer distances than I ought. I was ready to use it on Goff should he fall, but I hoped to save it for myself.

His climb was slower than Rennielle's had been, and I could feel the anxiety stretching between those of us below, like a web ready to catch him. At last there was a shuffling, and a knock. The door above opened and let blue light in once more. Then

Goff's form blocked it, there was an echoing thud, and the light disappeared again.

Harthor was already on the rope, and I could hear him moving upwards. My song grew louder in my throat. It was what I always did in times of stress, or so my companions thought. Another knock, another light, another descent into darkness. Imerian found my hand in the dark and squeezed it before he stepped onto my bent knee and cupped hands. I couldn't speak, just sing, and by now the tune was echoing up the chimney and through my body. I let a little — just a tiny bit of it — seep from my vibrating hands into Imerian's foot as I pushed him upwards.

And then I waited while he climbed, knocked, and left me alone in the dark. My song was at full force now. I reached up and stopped the dangling leather cord from swinging. I had to let go to bend my knees, though. With one hand in the air for direction, I squatted almost to the ground and sprang.

My jump propelled me upward like a startled cat. I lost track of the cord, but felt the knot at the end of the rope hit me in the back. I flailed, reaching behind to grab at it, and tumbled in slow motion, bashing my knees and then my head against the walls of the chimney. Sparks filled my eyes, but somehow my hand found the flying leather cord and hung on.

I weighed so little now that I didn't yank my shoulder out of its home or snap the cord as I descended. Instead I floated like cottonwood fluff in a spring breeze. My panicked flailing had stopped the song in my throat, but the effect lingered, and I pulled myself up the rope as easily as drawing laundry in on the line.

I didn't take the hand Imerian offered as I climbed through the trap door. I was still unwilling to admit my arcane abilities to these comrades I'd known for less than a month, and I didn't want him to feel how light I was. I dusted myself off and looked around the dimly lit cellar while Imerian pulled up the rope to retrieve his leather cord. From the layers of cobwebs and the faltering light of the aged evenlamp on the wall, it seemed the place was not in use as a storehouse for wine any longer. However, tracks in the dust led to the stone stairs at the end of the vaulted chamber. "Are those yours?" I asked the others.

Rennielle and Harthor shook their heads. Goff was still leaning against a broken wooden cask, breathing heavily.

The Essaruk woman had implied that servants and villagers used this exit unbeknownst to the garrison. There was nothing for it but to hope that was true. I nodded my readiness to go on, and we followed the tracks to the stairs. The corridor on the other side was deserted, and only slightly less dusty than the cellar. The air had a cold, unused smell, and I took comfort in the hope the garrison was not using this part of the keep.

There were no evenlamps here, only small lights from pigeon-inhabited windlets in the wall. These were useful, in that they told us direction. No light would come from the west side, which was sunk in the mountain's flank. Alert, nervous, feeling every rasping breath from Goff, we moved along the corridor like ghosts in the castle.

"It's my fault," Goff wheezed as we rested for a moment at the end of the long passageway.

"Sh!" said Rennielle sharply. I ignored her. There were no people here—I could feel it in the air.

"What is?" The climb up the rope had taken its toll on Goff, and he hadn't recovered. Just the walk down the corridor had winded him all over again.

"Olenbry ... I slept next to her ... as ... she died." Each word cost him effort.

Imerian put a hand on Goff's shoulder. "Death in the night is a silent blessing. Would you rob her of that peaceful end? If anyone is to blame, it is I. If I hadn't given her willow bark, or if I had woken for my watch, I may have been able to save her."

"If you had been woken," I corrected him. "We are all exhausted. No one could be expected to wake up on their own." I didn't look at Rennielle, who had left her post to chase Dortallah.

"We should keep moving," Harthor said. "We're fortunate to have been given this route through the keep. Let's not squander it."

Goff was leaning against the wall, hands on his thighs, head down.

"I don't think he can," I said. I looked at Imerian. "Is there anything at all you can do?"

He shook his head. "I've exhausted my supplies. I have nothing left I can safely give him."

"What about unsafely?" croaked Goff. "It's either that or leave me behind with her." He waved his hand, presumably at the ghost of Olenbry. I hoped he was being metaphorical and not actually hallucinating. I cursed my grandmother. If only she had taught me to sing healing charms. If only I hadn't run away before I was too young to use them safely ...

"What do you mean?" I turned to Imerian. "What does he mean, 'unsafely'?"

"I have two doses of *nîask*."

There was an intake of breath from Harthor, and Rennielle's head snapped around like a raptor's, focussing on Goff.

"And you knew this? Why not give it to Olenbry?"

"She was only half Ilvani. It would simply have accelerated her disease and killed her sooner."

"Goff is not any part Ilvani," I said. "And yet you're contemplating giving it to him. What is it?"

"I've trained my body to it," Goff whispered. "Tiny amounts, over time."

Harthor interrupted. "It's the poison Valnirati warriors take before battle. It makes them stronger, faster, less bothered by pain. Many die glorious deaths."

"Not all warriors," said Rennielle. "Most prefer to rely on their own skill and strength, and live to fight another day."

"Give me the vial," said Goff. "I won't use it unless I have to."

Imerian shook his head. "It's safer if I administer it."

Goff held out a shaking hand. "I'm not going to ask you to do that, my friend. Give it to me. That's an order."

Imerian took a small glass bottle from his pouch. "You're in no fit state to be giving orders, Goffree, but since it belongs to you, I'm giving it back. Please don't use it."

There was a lump in my throat as I watched the exchange, and I felt the ghost of Olenbry circling round us.

"Thank you," said Goff, and he held the small bottle up to the dim light from the pigeonholes. With a movement swifter than I thought him capable, he uncapped it and upended it on his tongue.

There was a collective 'no' from us all, but before Imerian's hand could snatch it away, Goff had restoppered the bottle.

"Just a drop," he said with a weak smile, and held up the vial, hardly less full. "Let's get out of this damned country."

VERSE 9

GOFFREE

At first there seemed to be no effect from the drug. Goff's breath still rasped like leaky bellows. But then, though his breath still rattled, his steps grew quicker and his back straighter. Through the length of the next passageway he moved ahead till he was abreast with Rennielle. She paused, put an arm out, and stopped us all in our tracks.

"What are you doing?"

He grasped her outstretched hand and kissed it, bending at the waist with a flourish I hadn't seen from him since our days at the Bastion.

"Leading us out of here, milady."

She snatched her hand away. "I am not your lady, and I can't hear what's ahead with you wheezing and tromping next to me."

"The *nîask* has made my eyes and ears as sharp as yours, my beauty. We are approaching the inhabited part of the stronghold. If any of us should venture into danger first, it should be me."

Rennielle looked as if she were about to argue, or to slap him.

"We haven't much time," Imerian murmured.

"Let him," I said at the same time. I knew that fervour in his eyes. If it was chemically enhanced, there would be no arguing with him anyway.

Another flight of stairs led us to a warm part of the keep, where the walls no longer wept and the smell of smoke and sweat and stale food flavoured the air. The door at the landing was barred from the other side.

"Do we wait for someone to open it by chance? Or try the other route?" Harthor asked. There had been another corridor, partly blocked with rubble and thick icicles, two flights of stairs down.

"Neither," said Goff. I ducked reflexively as he lunged forward, wielding his sword backward like an axe. With inhuman speed and fury, he splintered a wood plank with the crossguard then hammered at it with the pommel. The wood gave way under the onslaught, and he casually reached his arm through the broken door to lift the bar.

And then he bellowed as a wash of boiling liquid hit the door. He stumbled inward, dragging the ruined door open as he pulled his arm free. We followed him into a kitchen. The cook who had thrown the kettle of soup, and a pair of scullery boys holding knives, fled through the far door, yelling, no doubt, for help.

Goff, the manic glint still alight in his eye, waved his sword. "After them." He sprinted out the door.

The rest of us spared a glance at each other. Imerian shook his head, and Rennielle's face was grimmer than usual. There was no time to argue strategy as we set off after him at a run. All we could do was hope to keep up with the drug-fuelled man before he ran into the reinforcements the kitchen staff were calling for.

Rennielle and I were the fittest, and our longer legs carried us away from the men, but we were no match for the *nîask* in Goff's veins. His sprint took him into the main hall of the keep. With a zing and a thud, a crossbow bolt embedded itself in the floorboard Goff's running foot had just departed. I threw my sword arm out, preventing Imerian and Harthor from following into the hall, and with my other hand I grabbed Rennielle by the shoulder, dragging her back to the shelter of the doorway. She shook me off angrily, but retreated nonetheless.

The bolt had come from above our heads, where a gallery ran the width of the hall. If we crossed the room, we'd be in clear sight of the bowman. Or men. We could head left or right beneath the gallery, but we would be exposed the minute we moved forward. Goff stood in the doorway across the great hall from us. In front of him he held a partly armoured man — a soldier, or guard perhaps — and was resting his sword across the man's collar.

"There are two with crossbows, and a door behind them," Goff called to us. "Tell them to uncrank their bows or I'll slit their friend's throat."

Rennielle spoke in Essaruk, her voice echoing under the gallery.

"One has lowered his," said Goff. "Tell them to hold up their unloaded bows."

Rennielle spoke again.

"Now!" shouted Goff.

"Left and right," I whispered. "And hug the walls."

Harthor and I went right, and the other two left. While Goff and Rennielle had been speaking, I had strung my bow and nocked an arrow. I was nowhere near as good a shot as Rennielle, but I could at least provide cover. As we dashed along the side of the hall, I glanced up to see the two now-unarmed bowmen standing at the rail, each holding a bow in one hand and bolts in the other. I crossed into full view just as a third Essaruk stepped through the gallery door, a longbow in hand. She drew and loosed, her white-fletched arrow flying straight at Goff and his hostage.

I loosed my own arrow, which went wide, but Rennielle's struck her in the chest. No longer skirting the walls, we ran straight for the doorway, counting on the time it would take to reload the crossbows.

Goff was on the floor just through the door, the dead hostage pinned to him by a longbow shaft that went through the Essaruk's clavicle. Goff had dropped his sword and had his fist to his mouth. Imerian heaved the body away, and Goff staggered to his feet, ignoring the blood pouring from his shoulder. The vial of *nîask* in his hand hit the floor and spun, pointing the way down the corridor.

"Let me see that," said Imerian, pulling Goff's hand away from the wound on his shoulder.

"No time," snarled Goff, and waved Imerian off.

The seemingly casual motion sent the Woodkin careening into the opposite wall, but there was no anger in Imerian's eyes, only caution.

"Go, go. Go!" shouted Rennielle, loosing an arrow back into the large hall with each word.

I snatched up the *nîask* bottle from the floor — not looking to see, but knowing in my gut it was empty — before bolting down the corridor after the men. I did not insult Rennielle by calling for her to follow. Her legs were long and her judgement fair.

We were running blind, with no map or inkling of the architecture of the keep other than a sense that the mountain pass lay upward. As stairs appeared, Harthor took them and we followed, each time hoping to find an exit, until a final door led out onto the top of a wind-blasted tower.

Rennielle slammed the door behind her, leaning against it as we appraised our choices. The tower loomed over the narrow track of the mountain pass. We had come too high, and our path through the mountain was below us.

I peered over the edge. The stonework was rough and could provide toe and finger holds enough to climb down—but not for someone bleeding from the shoulder. There was no way out for Goff except back down the stairs.

Rennielle, who had her ear to the door, whispered, "They're coming."

"Then let them," growled Goff, reaching past her to open the door.

But Rennielle wouldn't budge. "Injured to the back, you fool."

"I'm a liability," he said. "Already wounded, and sick. The *nîask* won't last, but I'm faster and stronger than you all right now."

"Goff," I shouted over the wind. "I owe you—I pledged to save your skin." I switched my longsword to my left hand and drew my Ilvan sword—the one I'd stabbed him with a decade ago.

"You owe me your sword, Allaigna. I choose to have it at my back."

With that he wrenched open the door, sending Rennielle tumbling, and thrust his sword into the belly of the first Essaruk to reach the landing.

I had never fought a siege—only learned about such warfare from my tutors. But theory proved out, and indeed a single man can hold a spiral staircase against many. The widdershins curve of the descent let Goff's sword arm hold the wide space, while the ascending Essaruk were constrained by the pillar. I flattened myself against the outer wall, my sword covering his right flank, while Imerian's steel-tipped staff thrust at the heads and blades that appeared around the pillar. Rennielle and Harthor came behind, arrows nocked for the moment we reached the bottom.

Slipping in blood, tripping on bodies, we reached the causeway that would take us into the Ilmar at last. There were only three Essaruk holding it, but they all carried loaded crossbows. Goff turned to us, the fever still burning in his oak-brown eyes. "Wait," he said in a marriage between growl and whisper. "That is an order."

With that, he charged forward.

My first thought, for good or ill, was "I don't take orders any more." I sprinted after him, finding speed I had thought long spent, and threw my shoulder into the back of his hips. Down we both went, and two crossbow quarrels zipped over our heads. The third hit neither of us but struck the flat of my longsword, snapping it out of my grasp and sending it spinning across the cobbled bridge.

I rolled away from Goff, my hand still stinging, and found my feet. The movement carried me towards the Essaruk, who dropped their bows and surged forward with long-bladed pole-arms. Armed only with my Ilvan sword, I lunged low, hand held high, and let the sword's guard protect me as I thrust into his armpit. He continued his path towards me, notwithstanding the blade through his shoulder, and I had no choice but to let go and stumble sideways, unarmed, into the measure of his comrades.

I prepared to close with the nearer of the two, trying to get past the lethal blade on the end of her polearm. But Goff, somehow back on his feet, shouldered into her, slamming her against her comrade, and in the same inhuman movement, he grasped my sword from the body of the first. With his own sword in one hand and mine in the other, he'd sliced open the neck of one Essaruk and thrust the other through the eye by the time our three companions reached us.

He turned, saluted me with my sword, and tossed it in the air. "Thank you," he growled as I caught it by the hilt.

I was still standing, transfixed by his prowess, when Imerian pressed my longsword back into my hand. It lurched me into motion, and the five of us headed down the causeway as fast as our ill, injured, and aching bodies could run.

There was no pursuit. Either the stronghold was too lightly garrisoned, or they were unconcerned now that we were fleeing — as unlikely as that seemed given the number we had killed or wounded. Still, we ran, leaving the road after the first turn and limping, stumbling, and falling down scree slopes and sparse, snag-ridden copses. When we stopped, the tower of the keep had disappeared behind the snow-topped trees, and the forest was thick around us.

I looked at us, blood- and mud-soaked, tattered and winded. But alive. We didn't speak at first, just gasped for air, Goff's rasping lungs loudest of all until, with a choking wheeze, he collapsed to the ground.

We could have hacked off some tree branches to make a litter, but even without the threat of Essaruk pursuit, night itself was closing on our heels. Instead we sat Goff on his own cloak and took it in turns to carry him between a pair of us as we headed down the mountain. The sun appeared briefly from under the snow-laden clouds before we sank beneath its sight. The cold of the shadows felt all the deeper after the short, welcoming glow.

Goff slipped in and out of consciousness as we went. Imerian had bound his wounded shoulder, but there was a worrying amount of blood soaking his entire left side. Too little of it was Essaruk, I felt sure. When he was awake he shivered, though his skin was so hot I could feel it just from carrying him. And when he slept, his bronze skin was ashen, even in the warm light of the brief sunset.

With the adrenaline of battle gone, we were cold, exhausted, feeling our own injuries, and error-prone. Twice we started down false paths that both Imerian and I should have noticed sooner, and many times we stumbled.

"Put me down," said Goff, who jolted awake when I fell to one knee.

"I'm fine," I said, regaining my feet. "Go back to sleep."

He struggled within the hammock of his cloak, trying to pull himself upward. Imerian, who was holding the bottom of the cloak, gently lowered Goff's legs to the ground. "The light is gone," he said. "We might as well rest."

I crouched, easing Goff's shoulders against my knees. The trees were dense here, and no snow covered the ground. I struggled out of my gloves to feel Goff's forehead, which was no longer hot but alarmingly cold.

He reached across his shoulder and grasped my hand in his. "Allaigna, let me see you."

I shrugged the pack from my shoulders and put it under his head in place of my aching knees.

"I promised your grandfather I'd look after my comrades before I knew you'd be one of them. I don't think I can keep that promise any longer."

A tiny flare of anger warmed my chest at the presumption of the men in my life who were supposedly looking after me. But it was an old, tired flame, with not enough air to do more than sputter.

"I owe you my sword, remember? It's I who have the debt."

He tried to shake his head, but it manifested as mere twitch.

A light bloomed behind me. Imerian had wound a match string around a dry branch for a makeshift torch.

The warm flame sent sharp shadows across Goff's face, accentuating the drawn flesh and mottled skin. He was always so beautiful, like a statue of the heroic age, with his dark curls, thick lashes, and sensuous mouth. An Ilmari prince, whether our family acknowledged him or not. That face, his true face, flicked in and out of sight with the gusts of wind that drew the flame. Was this what my grandmother's Sight was like, I wondered? Unbidden magic that comes and goes as it will?

Goff was struggling with something in his hands. I realized it was his rings. He tugged them off at last and pressed the plain iron one into my hand. "You'll need this," he whispered. "For the map. And this," — the second one fell from his fingers, landing like a feather in my palm — "belongs in the family."

I held it up to the light. It was a signet, with the falcon of Brandishear. I couldn't read the inscription in the dim glow of the torch, but I felt certain the ring had belonged to Girondrey Brandis, my grandfather's older brother, and before him perhaps to Prince High Goffree.

I would not argue with him now. I slipped the signet onto my index finger and the iron ring onto my thumb.

"Stop them, cuz," he said, his voice barely audible over the wind in the trees. "You're the only one who has the right."

§

Find out what happens next in **Allaigna's** *Song:* Chorale, *the conclusion to the Allaigna's Song trilogy, due out in November 2021 from Pulp Literature Press.*

THE ARTISTS

Tatjana Mirkov-Popovicki
Cover artist, Helby Island Afternoon

Tatjana Mirkov-Popovicki is an award-winning Canadian landscape painter and writer based in Port Moody, British Columbia, where she settled after emigrating from Serbia in 1994. Although art was her first and true love, the challenging reality of her native country made her choose education in science. She graduated with a BSc in Electrical Engineering and pursued a high-tech career while studying and making art part-time. Tatjana is now a full-time painter with a passion for the West Coast and mountains. She is a past president, senior signature artist (SFCA), and honourable lifetime member of the Federation of Canadian Artists. Her paintings have been exhibited, collected, and represented by art galleries since 2005.

Tatjana also writes literary short stories about characters from Serbia and Canada. Her work has won awards in Canada and has been published in literary magazines in the US, UK, and Ireland. Tatjana's short story 'Afterlife' won *Pulp Literature*'s 2019 Hummingbird Flash Fiction Prize, and appears in Issue 25, Winter 2020. She is working on a collection of stories set in Tito's Yugoslavia, featuring a bigger-than-life heroine named Bistra. Please visit her website mirkov-popovicki.com to see her art and to find out more about her writing journey.

Matthew Nielsen
Artist, 'Houses'
Matthew Nielsen (aka Nuclear Jackal) is a comic artist currently working on *Toni & Aberdeen*, a graphic novel about two time travellers living in an empty 2003 Vancouver. He has illustrated Monstercat's *8 Year Anniversary* comic and David Edwards's *The Cold and Actual Sky* and *Forever the Star Finder*. His own comics have appeared in *BANG! Magazine*, *Sequential Magazine*, and two Cloudscape Comics anthologies (plus a zine about bees). He has also created merchandise artwork for both Military History Visualized and Military Aviation History. His story, 'The Endless Drop', inked by Minna Hakkola, appeared in Issue 22, Spring 2019, of *Pulp Literature*.

Matthew was raised by a Danish father and a Canadian mother in a Welsh port town. He was identified with special needs from a young age and eventually diagnosed with Asperger's Syndrome at age eleven. He was expelled from secondary school at twelve, then went to a school for violent teenagers. He was told he was the first person educated there to pass a national exam, and went on to college and then university, where he graduated with a degree in Illustration. 'Houses' is inspired by the many moves in his life. He now lives in Canada, and as of this writing is moving house again.

Mel Anastasiou
In-house illustrator
Mel Anastasiou loves drawing for *Pulp Literature* because she loves the stories she illustrates. She draws in black and white, working from imagination and inspired by details from Renaissance compositions. You can find illustrations, writing tips, and news about her books and novellas at melanastasiou.wordpress.com, and see more of her artwork on Facebook at Bird and Branch Artwork.

HALL OF FAME

In Memoriam

*It is with great sadness we say goodbye to our friend **Ariadne Bursewicz**. A longtime patron of the magazine, a wonderful writer, and a true lover of the written word, Ariadne passed away peacefully while reading in bed. Please join us in lifting a glass of your tipple of choice in her memory.*

These are the heroes — the Patrons and Pulp Literati whose monthly support helped bring you this issue. Please lift your glasses and give them a rousing cheer!

The Shareholders
Rapscallion

The Brewers
Robin McGillveray
A Bursewicz

The Landlords
Isabel Cushey
Dana Tye Rally

The Innkeepers
Ada Maria Soto
Margot Landels
Ev Bishop
Shannon Saunders
Roger & Anne Anastasiou
Kevin Harris
Gillian Gardiner
Megan Shaw
Susan Jackson
Meghan Dahl

The Cicerones
Elsa Carruthers

The Bartenders
Alana Krider
Richard Gropp
Ron Graves
Kristen Mah
Robert Bose
Victoria McAuley
Dave Wayne
Scott F Gray
Michelle Balfour
Abigail Bruce
Vernice Dietra Malik
Katriona Greenmoor
AD Bane
KT Wagner
Michael Weckworth
Deepthi Atukorala
Margot Spronk
Margaret Elliott

Peter Halasz
Bjarne Hansen
Leny Wagner
Kain Stewart
Chris Olee
kc dyer
Kimberley Aslett
Jan Fagan
Ken Oakes
Brighton Hugg
Alexa Benzaid-
Williams
Bryan Moose
Maureen Cooke
Lorna Keach
Katja Rammer

The Regulars
CC Humphreys
Marta Salek
Rina Piccolo
Emily Lonie

Jenny Blackford
Jain Cairns
Akemi Art
BC
Meredith Frazier
Catherine Levinson
Vera
Charity Tahmaseb
Alexander Langer
Marilyn Holt
Risa Wolf
Barbara Pengelly
David Perlmutter
Christine McCullough
Ishbel Newstead

The Clientele
Ray Hsu
Melissa Hudson

If you would like to join the ranks of these worthies, you can become a patron on Patreon at patreon. com/pulplit or join the Pulp Literati through our website at pulpliterature.com/join-pulp-literati/.

Have you heard?

Pulp Literature has a podcast!

Our podcast **The Pulp Lit Pulpit** is available on Podbean. The episodes are filled with editor advice, exclusive author interviews, and serialized story-time instalments from *Allaigna's Song: Overture* and *Stella Ryman and the Fairmount Manor Mysteries.*

Each episode has a limited lifespan of about eight to twelve weeks, after which it's gone! The episodes are available for download so you can save them for when you want to hear them most. **Find the latest episodes here:** pulpliterature.podbean.com

https://pulpliterature.com

@pulpliteraturepress

MARKETPLACE

ℬooks

Advent *by Michael Kamakana* · We thought we knew what the aliens wanted. Think again. · pulpliterature.com/advent

Allaigna's Song: Aria *by JM Landels* · The long-awaited sequel to the bestselling *Allaigna's Song* trilogy. ·pulpliterature.com/allaignas-song

The Extra: A Monument Studios Mystery *by Mel Anastasiou* · Extra Frankie Ray gets her big break on the Silver Screen, until Murder steals the scene. pulpliterature.com/the-extra

The Labours of Mrs Stella Ryman: Further Fairmount Mysteries *by Mel Anastasiou* · Trapped in a down-at-the-heels care home. You'd be cranky too. · pulpliterature.com/stella-ryman-and-the-fairmount-manor-mysteries

What the Wind Brings *by Matthew Hughes* · Winner of the 2020 Endeavour Award · pulpliterature.com/product-category/novels/matthew-hughes

The Writer's Boon Companion *by Mel Anastasiou* · Thirty Days Towards an Extraordinary Volume · pulpliterature.com/subscribe/the-bookstore

ℬookstores

Book Warehouse · 632 Broadway W, Vancouver, BC V5Z 1G1 · 604-872-5711 bookwarehouse.ca

Myth Hawker Travelling Bookstore · Canadian authors· Canadian content· small and independent press · mythhawker.ca

Phoenix On Bowen · 992 Dorman Rd, Bowen Island, BC V0N 1G0 · 604-947-2793

Village Books & Coffee House · 130-12031 First Ave, Richmond, BC V7E 3M1 · 604-272-6601 · villagebooks@shaw.ca

Western Sky Books · 2132-2850 Shaughnessy St, Port Coquitlam, BC V3C 6K5 · 604-461-5602 · store.westernskybooks.com

White Dwarf / Dead Write Books · 3715 10th Ave W, Vancouver, BC V6R 2G5 · 604-228-8223 · whitedwarf@deadwrite.com

ℭonferences and Events

When Words Collide · August 2021 Calgary, AB · whenwordscollide.org

Wine Country Writers' Festival 24–25 September 2021 · Penticton, BC winecountrywritersfestival.ca

Surrey International Writers' Conference 22–24 October 2021 · Virtual Event · siwc.ca

Word on the Lake · May 2022 · Salmon Arm, BC · wordonthelakewritersfestival.com

Creative Ink Festival · May 2022 Burnaby, BC · creativeinkfestival.com

Room's CONTEST CALENDAR
NOW WITH NEW DEADLINES!

Fiction Contest
1st Prize: $1,000 + publication
2nd Prize: $250 + publication
Deadline: March 8

Creative Non-Fiction Contest
1st Prize: $500 + publication
2nd Prize: $250 + publication
Deadline: June 1

Poetry Contest
1st Prize: $1,000 + publication
2nd Prize: $250 + publication
Deadline: August 15

Short Forms Contest
1st Prize: $500 + publication *(two awarded)*
Deadline: November 1

Entry Fee: $35 CAD ($42 USD for International entries).
Entry includes a one-year subscription to *Room*. Additional entries $7.
Visit roommagazine.com/contests.

For more information on our contests
and upcoming calls for submissions,
visit roommagazine.com.

Room
LITERATURE, ART, AND FEMINISM SINCE 1975

Do you have a **story to tell?**
We can help!

Dreamers is dedicated to heartfelt writing. Visit our site for:

- Therapeutic Writing
- Poems & Stories
- Content Marketing
- Creative Nonfiction
- Writing Workshops
- Contests & Anthologies
- Residencies & Retreats
- ...and so much more!

www.DreamersWriting.com

GEIST
Keep it weird.
Subscribe today!
go to geist.com/subscribe
or call 1-888-GEIST-EH
LOST CITY
FACT + FICTION ● NORTH of AMERICA

on spec
the canadian magazine of the fantastic
Expect the unexpected.
www.onspec.ca

HELP WANTED ?

If you are a new writer, or a writer with a troublesome manuscript,
EVENT's **Reading Service for Writers**
may be just what you need.

Manuscripts will be edited by one of EVENT's editors and receive an assessment of 700-1000 words, focusing on such aspects of craft as voice, structure, rhythm and point of view.

eventmagazine.ca

The casting call is murder

COMING SOON FROM

PULP LITERATURE PRESS

Magazines

Amazing Stories · Back in print!
amazingstories.com

The Digest Enthusiast · Digests past and present plus new genre fiction larquepress.com

EVENT Magazine · Poetry and prose eventmagazine.ca

Geist Ideas + Culture·Made in Canada geist.com

Mystery Weekly Magazine The cutting edge of short mystery fiction www.mysteryweekly.com

Neo-opsis · Canadian magazine of science fiction based in Victoria, BC · neo-opsis.ca

OnSpec · The Canadian magazine of the fantastic · onspecmag.wordpress.com

Polar Borealis · Paying market for new Canadian SF&F writers & artists · polarborealis.ca

Room Magazine · Literature, Art, and Feminism since 1975 · roommagazine.com

Printing & Publishing

First Choice Books/Victoria Bindery Book printing & binding · graphic design · eBooks · marketing materials 1-800-957-0561 · firstchoicebooks.ca

Writing Resources

Dreamers Creative Writing · Workshops, residencies, contests, and more! · www. dreamerswriting.com

Quit the Day Job · A school for writers from Pulp Literature Press pulpliterature.com/quit-the-day-job

The Writers' Lodge on Bowen Island The Muse retreats for writers · pulpliterature.com/calendar-of-events/retreats/

NEO-OPSIS
Science Fiction Magazine
www.neo-opsis.ca

PULP
Literature

Become a member!

Join the Pulp Literati today
pulpliterature.com/join-pulp-literati

"Myth Hawker has a crush on the underdog: the small press, the overlooked author, the independent bookstore, and the vast, undiscovered treasures of small-scale publishing."

Myth Hawker travels the length & breadth of Canada, popping up at conventions & festivals in every province, showcasing the work of small press & independent Canadian authors. Follow them online to see where they're popping up next!

www.mythhawker.com @Mythhawker

NEW FROM
PULP LITERATURE
PRESS

*Allaigna's Song
Aria*

BY JM LANDELS

THE HIGHLY
ANTICIPATED
SEQUEL TO THE
BESTSELLING

*Allaigna's Song
Overture*

*You can't escape magic
when it's in your blood*

pulpliterature.com

The Labours of Mrs Stella Ryman
Further Fairmount Manor Mysteries

When the machineries of institution fail to protect Fairmount Manor, octogenarian amateur sleuth Mrs Stella Ryman rolls up her fleece jacket sleeves to ferret out a thief, investigate a gun-toting resident, set right a mishandled investigation of a man's death, pursue spectres and footpads walking at midnight, and discover Thelma Hu's long-lost fortune.

Book II of the Fairmount Manor Mysteries by Mel Anastasiou, available now from Pulp Literature Press

PULPLITERATURE.COM/STELLA-RYMAN
ISBN (PRINT): 978-1-988865-11-9
ISBN (EBOOK): 978-1-988865-12-6

CONTESTS

Pulp Literature runs four annual contests for poetry, flash fiction, and short stories. For contest guidelines, prizes, and entry fees, see pulpliterature.com/contests.

The Raven Short Story Contest
Contest opens: 1 September 2021
Deadline: 15 October 2021
Winner notified: 15 November 2021
Winner published: Issue 34, Spring 2022
Prize: $300

The Bumblebee Flash Fiction Contest
Contest opens: 1 January 2022
Deadline: 15 February 2022
Winner notified: 15 March 2022
Winner published: Issue 35, Summer 2022
Prize: $300

The Magpie Award for Poetry
Contest opens: 1 March 2022
Deadline: 15 April 2022
Winner notified: 15 May 2022
Winner published: Issue 36, Autumn 2022
Prize: $500

The Hummingbird Flash Fiction Prize

Contest opens: 1 May 2022

Deadline: 15 June 2022

Winner notified: 15 July 2022

Winner published: Issue 37, Winter 2023

Prize: $300

$\mathscr{B}$ecome a $\textsc{Patron}$ of $\textsc{Pulp Literature}$

By supporting *Pulp Literature* on Patreon with $2 or more per month, you will be laying the foundation for a secure future for the magazine, as well as ensuring that you never miss an issue! Your subscription includes four big issues of short stories, novellas, poetry, comics, and novel excerpts, delivered to your door or electronic mailbox each year. **Find us at patreon.com/pulplit**

If you prefer to subscribe through our website, go to pulpliterature.com/subscribe.

Or you can send a cheque with the form below to
Subscriptions, Pulp Literature Press, 21955 16 Ave, Langley BC, V2Z 1K5, Canada

----

Don't miss an issue!

- ❏ **Send me 2 years (8 issues) at the special rate of $90** (save $30)*
- ❏ **Send me 1 year (4 issues) for $50** (save $10)*
- ❏ **Send me 2 years of digital issues for $30** (save $9.92)
- ❏ **Send me 1 year of digital issues for $17.50** (save $2.47)

Name: ____

Address: ____

City: _______________________________ Prov. / State: __________

Postal code: ______________ Country: ___________________

Email: ____

- ❏ **Payment enclosed**
- ❏ **Bill me**
- ❏ **New**
- ❏ **Renewal**

Make cheques payable in Canadian funds to J. Landels. Include email address for digital editions and Paypal billing, or subscribe at www.pulpliterature.com.

*for postage outside Canada add $20 per year in North America or $36 per year overseas.

www.ingramcontent.com/pod-product-compliance
Lightning Source LLC
Chambersburg PA
CBHW061255210726

48293CB00003B/978